The Marquis de Sade

Born in 1740 and educated at a Jesuit school in Paris, Donatien Alphonse François, Marquis de Sade, served as a cavalry officer in the Seven Years' War against Prussia. After his discharge from the royal army in 1763, his life was punctuated by violent scandals over his sexual conduct and by feuds with his enemies. His lurid career encompassed the brutalization of prostitutes, trials for murder and sexual offenses, condemnations to death, dramatic escapes from prison, a public affair with his wife's sister, and lengthy incarcerations at Vincennes and the Bastille. A man in constant revolt against the sexual, social, and political values of his day, Sade spent twenty-eight of his last forty years in prison. In 1803 the government had Sade committed to the insane asylum at Charenton, where he wrote and produced plays—basing the characters on his fellow inmates—until his death in 1814.

Because of their pornographic and blasphemous subject matter, approximately one-fourth of Sade's manuscripts were burned by the police during the Consulate and the Empire, and most of the rest were denied official publication by the French courts until the late 1950s. Although his most radical works, such as the infamous *120 Days of Sodom* (1785), his masterpiece *Justine* (1791), and the subversive *Philosophy of the Bedroom* (1795), are still considered by many to be obscene, the writings of the Marquis de Sade have had a profound influence not only on the development of erotic literature but also on some of the great modern philosophers of individual liberty, including Nietzsche, Freud, Dostoevsky, and Kafka.

Ask your bookseller for Bantam Classics by these other international writers.

ARISTOPHANES
DANTE ALIGHIERI
FYODOR DOSTOEVSKY
ALEXANDRE DUMAS
EURIPIDES
GUSTAVE FLAUBERT
JOHANN WOLFGANG VON GOETHE
JACOB AND WILHELM GRIMM
HOMER
VICTOR HUGO
HENRIK IBSEN
FRANZ KAFKA
PIERRE CHODERLOS DE LACLOS
GASTON LEROUX
NICCOLO MACHIAVELLI
THOMAS MANN
KARL MARX AND FRIEDRICH ENGELS
PLATO
EDMOND ROSTAND
SOPHOCLES
MARIE-HENRI BEYLE DE STENDHAL
LEO TOLSTOY
IVAN TURGENEV
JULES VERNE
VIRGIL
VOLTAIRE
JOHANN WYSS

The Crimes of Love

3 Novellas by the Marquis de Sade

(Donatien Alphonse François, Marquis de Sade)

Translated by Lowell Bair
With an Introductory Note by
Aldous Huxley

BANTAM BOOKS

New York · Toronto · London · Sydney · Auckland

THE CRIMES OF LOVE
A Bantam Classic Book
PUBLISHING HISTORY
First Bantam edition published in June 1964
Bantam Classic edition / September 1993

"The Dreamer (Summer Evening)," Jane S. Tissot.
National Portrait Gallery, London.

"A Note on the Marquis de Sade" is excerpted
from Ends and Means,
by Aldous Huxley. Copyright © 1937 by Aldous Huxley. Reprinted
by permission of the Estate of Aldous Huxley.

ISBN 0-553-21424-1

Published simultaneously in the United States and Canada

Bantam Books are published by Bantam Books, a division of
Bantam Doubleday Dell Publishing Group, Inc. Its trademark,
consisting of the words "Bantam Books" and the portrayal of
a rooster, is Registered in U.S. Patent and Trademark Office
and in other countries. Marca Registrada. Bantam Books,
1540 Broadway, New York, New York 10036.

PRINTED IN THE UNITED STATES OF AMERICA

OPM   0 9 8 7 6 5

Contents

significance in the world? Was his intellect more piercing than that of other men? Was he forced by the acuity of his vision to look through the veils of prejudice and superstition to the hideous reality behind them? We may doubt it. The real reason why the Marquis could see no meaning or value in the world is to be found in those descriptions of fornications, sodomies and tortures which alternate with the philosophizings of *Justine* and *Juliette*. In the ordinary circumstances of life, the Marquis was not particularly cruel; indeed, he is said to have got into serious trouble during the Terror for his leniency towards those suspected of anti-revolutionary sentiments. His was a strictly sexual perversion. It was for flogging actresses, sticking pen-knives into shop girls, feeding prostitutes on sugar-plums impregnated with cantharides, that he got into trouble with the police. His philosophical disquisitions, which, like the pornographic day-dreams, were mostly written in prisons and asylums, were the theoretical justification of his erotic practices. Similarly his politics were dictated by the desire to avenge himself on those members of his family and his class who had, as he thought, unjustly persecuted him. He was enthusiastically a revolutionary—at any rate in theory; for, as we have seen, he was too gentle in practice to satisfy his fellow Jacobins. His books are of permanent interest and value because they contain a kind of *reductio ad absurdum* of revolutionary theory. Sade is not afraid to be a revolutionary to the bitter end. Not content with denying the particular system of values embodied in the *ancien régime*, he proceeds to deny the existence of any values, any idealism, any binding moral imperatives whatsoever. He preaches violent revolution not only in the field of politics and economics, but (logical with the appalling logicality of the maniac) also on that of personal relations, including the most intimate of all, the relations between lovers. And, after all, why not? If it is legitimate to torment and kill in one set of circumstances, it must be equally legitimate to torment and kill in all other circumstances. De Sade is the one completely consistent and thorough-going revolutionary of history.

The Crimes
of Love

Eugénie de Franval

$\mathcal{T}$o instruct man and correct his morals: that is our only purpose in writing this story. We hope that reading it will make one keenly aware of the peril that always dogs the steps of those who stop at nothing in satisfying their desires. May they come to realize that a good upbringing, wealth, talents and gifts of nature are likely only to lead one astray unless they are supported or made effective by self-restraint, good conduct, wisdom and modesty. These are the truths we are going to illustrate. We ask to be forgiven for the monstrous details of the abominable crime we shall be forced to describe: it is not possible to make others detest such wrongdoing if one does not have the courage to lay it bare.

It is rare that everything combines in one person to bring him to complete well-being. If he is favored by nature, then fortune refuses him her gifts; if fortune lavishes her favors on him, then nature mistreats him. It seems that the Almighty wishes to show us that in each individual, as well as in His most sublime operations, the laws of equilibrium are the first laws of the universe, those which regulate everything that occurs, everything that vegetates, and everything that breathes.

Franval lived in Paris, where he had been born. In addition to an income of four hundred thousand francs a year, he had an extremely handsome face and figure, and a wide variety of talents. But beneath this attractive exterior were concealed all sorts of vices, including, unfortunately, those whose adoption and practice quickly

3

leads to crime. Franval's primary fault was a disorder of the imagination that exceeded all description. This is a fault which one does not correct; its effects increase as strength and vigor decline. The less one can do, the more one undertakes; the less one acts, the more one invents; and satiety, far from chilling one's ardor, paves the way for more vicious refinements.

As we have said, Franval was abundantly endowed with all the charms of youth and all the talents that embellish it; but he was so contemptuous of moral and religious duties that it had become impossible for his teachers to make him fulfill any of them.

In an age when the most dangerous books are in the hands of children as well as in those of their fathers and their tutors, and when rashness of thought passes for strength, and licentiousness passes for imagination, young Franval's wit aroused appreciative laughter; he might be scolded for it a moment afterward, but later he would be praised. His father, a zealous advocate of all the currently fashionable sophisms, was the first to encourage his son to think "soundly" upon all these matters. He himself lent him the books that were capable of corrupting him most rapidly. In view of this, what tutor would have dared to inculcate principles different from those of the household in which he was obliged to please?

Be that as it may, Franval lost his parents while he was still very young, and when he was nineteen an elderly uncle, who also died a short time later, arranged a marriage for him and gave him all the property that he was to have inherited some day.

With such a fortune, Monsieur de Franval could expect to encounter no difficulty in finding a wife. A multitude of matches were proposed, but he had begged his uncle to give him a girl younger than himself, with as few relatives as possible, and, to satisfy him, his uncle had directed his attention to a Mademoiselle de Farneille, a financier's daughter whose family now consisted only of her mother. She was quite young, only fifteen, but she had a very real income of sixty thousand francs a year and the most charming face in Paris, one of those virginal faces in which candor and sweetness are expressed by the delicate lineaments of love and all the feminine graces. She had lovely blond hair that hung down below her waist, big blue eyes filled with tenderness and modesty, a lithe and graceful figure, lily-white skin and the freshness of a rose. She was endowed with many talents, a lively but rather sad imagination, and a little of that gentle melancholy which makes one love books and solitude—attributes which nature seems to grant only to those whom she has destined to know adversity, as though to make it less bitter by the somber and deeply moving pleasure it brings them. This pleasure makes them prefer tears to the frivolous joy of happiness, which is much less active and penetrating.

Madame de Farneille was thirty-two at the time of her daughter's marriage. She, too, was intelligent and charming, but she had perhaps a little too much reserve and severity. Eager to assure the happiness of her only child, she had consulted everyone in Paris about her marriage. She no longer had any relatives and her only advisors were those cold friends to whom all things are alike. They convinced her that the young man who was being proposed for her daughter was without a doubt the best match she could find in Paris, and that it would be unforgivably foolish of her to miss such an opportunity. And so the wedding took place, and the young couple, rich enough to take a house of their own, established themselves in it within a few days.

Young Franval's character was free of those faults of levity, disorder and thoughtlessness which prevent a man from being fully developed before the age of thirty. Having complete confidence in himself, loving order and being thoroughly competent in the management of a household, he had all the qualities necessary for that aspect of a happy life. His faults, of an entirely different nature, were the vices of maturity rather than the indiscretions of youth: he was hypocritical, scheming, malicious, base, selfish, deceitful and extremely crafty, and he covered all this not only by the charms and talents we have already mentioned, but also by eloquence, great wit and a most attractive appearance. Such was the man with whom we shall be dealing.

As is customary, Mademoiselle de Farneille had known her husband no more than a month before their marriage. Deceived by his false qualities, she had become his dupe; the days were not long enough for the pleasure of contemplating him, she idolized him, and things reached the point where there would have been fear for her life if any obstacles had arisen to trouble the sweetness of a marriage in which, she said, she found her only happiness.

As for Franval, who was philosophical with regard to women as well as everything else in life, he considered that charming young lady with utter impassivity. "The woman who belongs to us," he said, "is someone whom custom places in bondage to us. She must be gentle, submissive and extremely virtuous—not that I share the common prejudice concerning the dishonor that a wife can inflict on us when she imitates our debauchery; it's only that no one likes to see someone else usurp his rights. Everything else is a matter of indifference; it adds nothing to happiness."

With such sentiments in a husband, it is easy to predict that life will not be a bed of roses for the poor girl who has married him. Upright, sensitive, well-bred, lovingly anticipating the desires of the only man in the world with whom she was concerned, Madame de Franval wore her chains for several years without becoming aware of her servitude. It was not difficult for her to see that her beloved husband was giving her only a few scraps of his tenderness, but she was so happy with the little he left her that she devoted all her efforts and attention to making sure that during those brief moments he would at least find everything she believed to be necessary for his enjoyment.

The best proof that Franval did not always shirk his duty, however, was that in the first year of their marriage his wife, then aged sixteen and a half, gave birth to a daughter who was even more beautiful than her mother. He immediately named her Eugénie—Eugénie, the horror and the wonder of nature.

Monsieur de Franval, who had no doubt formed the most odious designs on this child as soon as she was born, separated her from her mother at once. Until the age of seven, Eugénie was in the hands of women on whom he could rely. They limited their care to giving her a good disposition and teaching her to read; they scrupulously avoided giving her any knowledge of the religious and moral principles in which girls of that age are usually instructed.

Madame de Farneille and her daughter, deeply

shocked by this conduct, reproached Monsieur de Franval for it. He calmly replied that since his plan was to make his daughter happy he did not want to instill in her any of those illusions which served no purpose except to frighten people without ever being useful to them, and that a girl, who needed to learn only how to be attractive, could do very well without such fantastic nonsense, for it would only trouble the serenity of her life and would not add any truth to her mind or any beauty to her body.

These words were extremely displeasing to Madame de Farneille. She was drawn more closely toward heavenly ideas as she moved further away from the pleasures of this world. Piety is a weakness inherent in advancing age or declining health. In the tumult of the passions, we usually feel very little anxiety over a future which we believe to be remote, but when the language of those passions becomes less imperious, when we are approaching the end, when everything begins to leave us, then we fall back on the God we heard about in our childhood. If, according to philosophy, these second illusions are as fantastic as the others, they are at least not so dangerous.

Franval's mother-in-law no longer had any relatives, and she herself had little influence; as we have already said, she had only a few of those casual friends who slip away from us if we put them to the test. Having to struggle against a young, charming son-in-law of high rank, she sensibly decided that it would be better to limit herself to remonstrances, rather than attempting to take more forceful measures with a man who would ruin her and have her daughter placed in confinement if they dared to oppose him. A few protests were therefore all she ventured, and she fell silent as soon as she saw that they had no effect. Franval, sure of his superiority and clearly aware that he was feared, soon ceased to restrain himself in any way. Contenting himself with casting a thin veil over his activities, merely because of the public, he moved straight toward his horrible goal.

As soon as Eugénie had reached the age of seven, Franval took her to his wife. That loving mother, who had not seen her child since giving birth to her, could not get her fill of caressing her; she held her against her bosom for two hours, covering her with kisses and bathing her in her tears. She wanted to become acquainted with her little talents, but Eugénie had none except reading fluently, enjoying robust health and being as beautiful as an angel. Madame de Franval was again plunged into despair when she recognized that it was all too true that her daughter did not know even the most elementary principles of religion.

"What, monsieur!" she said to her husband. "Are you bringing her up only for this world? Won't you please reflect that she, like everyone else, will live in it only a short time, and will then enter into an eternity that will be terrible for her if you deprive her of everything she needs in order to enjoy happiness at the feet of the Being who gave her life."

"If Eugénie knows nothing, madame," replied Franval, "if those maxims have been carefully concealed from her, she can't be unhappy because of it, for if they're true, the Supreme Being is too just to punish her for her ignorance, and if they're false, what need is there to tell her about them? As for the rest of her education, please rely on me: from now on I'm going to be her tutor, and I promise you that within a few years she'll surpass all other children of her age."

Madame de Franval insisted. She called on the

eloquence of the heart to assist that of reason and her tears expressed themselves for her, but Franval was unmoved by them and did not seem even to notice them. He had Eugénie taken away and told his wife that if she tried to interfere in any way with the education he intended to give their daughter, or if she suggested to her any principles different from those on which he was going to nurture her, she would be depriving herself of the pleasure of seeing her, and he would send Eugénie to one of his castles, which she would never leave. Madame de Franval, accustomed to submission, yielded to him; she begged him not to separate her from her beloved daughter and promised, weeping, that she would do nothing to disturb the education that was being prepared for her.

Mademoiselle de Franval was immediately placed in a very beautiful apartment adjoining her father's, with a highly intelligent governess, an assistant governess, a chambermaid and two little girls of her own age, intended solely for her amusement. She was given teachers of writing, drawing, poetry, natural history, elocution, geography, astronomy, anatomy, Greek, English, German, Italian, fencing, dancing, riding and music. She got up every morning at seven o'clock, no matter what the season. She went out into the garden and ate a big piece of rye bread which formed her entire breakfast. She came back inside at eight o'clock and spent a few moments in her father's apartment while he frolicked with her or taught her little parlor games. She prepared for her lessons until nine o'clock, when her first teacher arrived. She received five of them, until two o'clock. She ate lunch with her governess and her two little friends. The meal was composed of vegetables, fish, pastry and fruit; there was never any meat, soup, wine, liqueurs or coffee. Between three and four o'clock, she went back to the garden to play with her friends. They played court tennis, ball, battledore and shuttlecock, and ninepins, and sometimes they practiced running and jumping. They dressed comfortably, according to the weather. Nothing constricted their waists; they were never enclosed in those ridiculous corsets which are equally dangerous to the stomach and to the chest, and which, hampering a young girl's breathing, necessarily attack her lungs. From four to six, Eugénie received more teachers, and since they could not all come on the same day, the others came the following day. Three times a week she went to the theater with her father; they sat in little grilled boxes which he rented for her by the year. At nine o'clock she came back and had dinner. She was served only vegetables and fruit. From ten to eleven, four times a week, she played with her governesses and her maid, read a novel and then went to bed. On the three other days, when Franval did not dine away from home, she was alone with him in his apartment, and this time was devoted to what he called his "lectures." He instilled in her his views on morality and religion; on the one hand, he presented to her what certain men thought about these matters, and, on the other, he set forth what he himself accepted.

Considering that Eugénie had great intelligence, broad knowledge, a quick mind and passions that were already becoming ignited, it is not difficult to imagine the progress these views made in her soul. But since the infamous Franval's goal was not merely to strengthen her mind, his lectures seldom ended without inflaming her heart; and that horrible man had succeeded so well in pleasing his daughter, he corrupted her so skillfully, made himself so useful to her education and her pleasures, and so ardently anticipated everything that might be agreeable to her, that in the midst of the most brilliant company she found no one as charming as her father. Even before he had stated his intentions openly, he had filled that weak and innocent creature's young heart with all those feelings of friendship, gratitude and tenderness which must necessarily lead to the most ardent love. She saw no one but him in the world, she paid no attention to anyone else, and she rebelled at the idea of anything that might separate her from him. She would gladly have given him not her honor, not her charms—those sacrifices would have seemed to her too slight for the soul-stirring object of her idolatry—but her blood, her life itself, if that tender friend of her heart had demanded it of her.

It was not the same with her feelings for her respectable and unhappy mother. Her father, by adroitly telling her that Madame de Franval, being his wife, demanded certain attentions of him which often prevented him from doing everything his heart dictated to him for his dear Eugénie, had found a way of engendering in her soul much more hatred and jealousy than the kind of respectful and tender feelings that she ought to have had for such a mother.

"My friend, my brother," she sometimes said to Franval, who did not want her to address him any differently, "that woman you call your wife, that creature who, according to you, brought me into the world, is very demanding, because by always wanting to have you with her, she deprives me of the happiness of spending all my time with you. . . . It's obvious that you prefer her to your Eugénie. For my part, I'll never love someone who takes your heart away from me."

"No, my dear," replied, Franval, "No one in the world will ever acquire rights over me as strong as yours. The ties between that woman and your best friend are only the fruit of custom and social convention; philosophically viewed by me, they will never counterbalance those which bind you and me together. You'll always be preferred, Eugénie; you'll always be the angel and the light of my life, the focus of my soul and the reason for my existence."

"Oh, how sweet those words are!" said Eugénie. "Repeat them often, my friend. . . . If you only knew how pleased I am by those expressions of your tenderness!" She took his hand and pressed it to her heart. "Yes, I feel them all here. . . ."

"Your tender caresses assure me that it's true," said Franval, clasping her in his arms. . . . And thus, without the slightest remorse, the crafty wretch made his final preparations for the poor girl's seduction.

Eugénie had just reached her fourteenth year, and this was the time when Franval had decided to consummate his crime. Let us shudder! He did it. . . .

They returned to Paris afterward, but the criminal pleasures in which that perverse man had reveled had so delightfully gratified his physical and moral faculties that his inconstancy, which had sooner or later put an end to all his other affairs, was unable to have any effect on this one. He fell madly in love with Eugénie, and this dangerous passion inevitably made him cruelly forsake his wife. Alas, what a victim! Madame de Franval, aged thirty-one at that time, was at the height of her beauty. An impression of sadness, a necessary result of the sorrows with which she was consumed, made her still more appealing. Bathed in her own tears, deep in the lassitude of melancholy, with her beautiful hair carelessly scattered over her alabaster bosom and her lips lovingly pressed against the cherished portrait of her faithless husband

and tyrant, she resembled one of those lovely virgins whom Michelangelo depicted in the depths of grief. But she had not yet learned the facts that would later complete her torment. The manner in which Eugénie was being educated; the essential things of which she was being left in ignorance, or of which she was being informed in such a way as to make her hate them; the certainty that those duties, despised by Franval, would never be permitted to her daughter; the little time that she was allowed to spend with Eugénie; the fear that the singular education she was being given would sooner or later lead to crime; Franval's dissoluteness; his daily harshness to her, when her only concern was to anticipate his wishes and her only delight was to interest or please him—such were, for the moment, the only causes of her distress. What painful shafts were going to pierce her tender, sensitive heart when she learned everything!

Meanwhile Eugénie's education continued; she herself had decided to go on with her lessons until she was sixteen, and her talents, her broad knowledge, the charms that were developing in her every day—everything bound Franval more strongly to her. It was easy to see that he had never loved anyone as he loved her.

Nothing had been changed in Eugénie's schedule except the time of the lectures; these private conversations with her father took place much more often and lasted far into the night. Only the governess knew about their affair, and they had enough confidence in her not to fear her indiscretion.

There was also a change in Eugénie's meals: she now ate with her parents. In a house like Franval's, this meant that she was in a position to become acquainted with people and to be desired as a wife. Several men asked for her hand in marriage. Franval was sure of her heart and did not feel that there was any reason for him to be alarmed by all those proposals, but he had not sufficiently considered the possibility that they might eventually reveal everything.

In a conversation with her daughter—a favor which she desired greatly and seldom obtained—Madame de Franval told her that Monsieur de Colunce wanted to marry her.

"You already know him," she said. "He loves you, he's young and charming, he'll be rich some day, and he's waiting for your consent . . . only for your consent, my child. What will your answer be?"

Eugénie, surprised, blushed and replied that she did not yet feel any inclination toward marriage, but that her father could be consulted on the matter and that she would comply with his wishes.

Seeing no hidden motives in this reply, Madame de Franval waited patiently for a few days until she found an opportunity to speak to her husband. She then told him of the intentions expressed by young Colunce and his family, and of Eugénie's answer. Franval, of course, already knew everything; he made a rather inadequate effort to disguise his feelings.

"Madame," he said curtly, "let me insistently ask you not to concern yourself with Eugénie. From the care I've taken to keep her away from you, it must have been easy for you to see how much I wanted you to have nothing to do with her. I must renew my orders to you on that subject. You won't forget them again, will you?"

"But what shall I answer, monsieur, since the request has been addressed to me?"

"You'll say that I appreciate the honor, but that my daughter has congenital defects which make marriage out of the question for her."

"But she has no such defects, monsieur. Why deprive your only child of the happiness she could find in marriage?"

"Has marriage made you very happy, madame?"

"Not all wives have failed as I have in being unable to attach you to me." She sighed. "Or perhaps not all husbands are like you . . ."

"Wives are deceitful, jealous, imperious, coquettish or sanctimonious; husbands are treacherous, unfaithful, cruel or despotic—there's a summary of everyone on earth, madame. Don't expect to find a paragon."

"And yet everyone gets married."

"Fools and idlers do; a philosopher has said that one gets married only when one does not know what one is doing, or when one no longer knows what to do."

"Then you think that the human race should be allowed to die out?"

"Why not? A plant that produces only poison can't be rooted out too soon."

"Eugénie won't be grateful to you for your excessive sternness toward her."

"Has she shown any desire to marry this young man?"

"Your wish is her command; she said so herself."

"Very well, madame: it's my wish that you forget about that marriage."

And Monsieur de Franval left, after strictly forbidding his wife ever to mention the subject to him again.

Madame de Franval told her mother of the conversation she had had with her husband, and Madame de Farneille, more perceptive and more accustomed to the effects of the passions than her attractive daughter, immediately suspected that something unnatural was involved.

Eugénie saw her grandmother very little: no more than an hour at a time, on important occasions, and always in Franval's presence. Madame de Farneille, wishing to clear up the matter, sent word to Franval that she would like to spend the entire afternoon with her granddaughter in order to distract herself from a headache that was causing her great suffering. Franval replied irritably that although there was nothing Eugénie feared more than the vapors, he would take her to see her grandmother, but that she could not stay long, because she would have to go to a physics course that she was assiduously pursuing.

When he and Eugénie arrived at Madame de Farneille's house, she did not conceal her astonishment at his refusal of the proposed marriage.

"I can see no reason," she said, "why you shouldn't allow Eugénie herself to convince me of the defect which, according to you, must prevent her from being married."

"Whether that defect is real or not, madame," said Franval, a little surprised by his mother-in-law's determination, "the fact is that Eugénie's marriage would cost me a great deal, and I'm still too young to consent to such a sacrifice. When she's twenty-five, she can do as she pleases, but she mustn't count on me till then."

"And are your feelings the same, Eugénie?" asked Madame de Farneille.

"They're different in one way, madame," Eugénie said with great firmness. "My father has given me his permission to get married when I'm twenty-five, but I swear to you and to him that I will never take advantage of that permission. With my way of thinking, it would only make my life unhappy."

"At your age, mademoiselle, one has no way of thinking," said Madame de Farneille. "There's something extraordinary in all this, and I must find out what it is."

"I urge you to try, madame," said Franval, taking Eugénie away. "In fact, you'll do well to employ your clergy to help you discover the key to the riddle. And when you've made skillful use of all your resources, when you know the answer at last, please tell me whether I'm right or wrong to oppose Eugénie's marriage."

Franval's sarcastic remark about his mother-in-law's ecclesiastical advisors was aimed at an estimable man whom it is now time to introduce, since the sequence of events will soon show him in action.

He was the confessor of Madame de Farneille and her daughter, one of the most virtuous men in France. Honest, benevolent, full of candor and wisdom, Monsieur de Clervil was far from all the vices of his calling and had only gentle and useful qualities. A steadfast supporter of the poor, a sincere friend of the opulent, a consoler of the unfortunate, this worthy man combined all the gifts that make one charming with all the virtues that make one sensitive and sympathetic.

When he was consulted on the matter, Clervil sensibly replied that before coming to any decision they would have to discover Monsieur de Franval's reasons for opposing his daughter's marriage. Madame de Farneille made a few remarks suggesting the possibility of the affair that actually existed all too concretely, but the prudent confessor rejected this idea: finding it much too insulting to both Madame de Franval and her husband, he indignantly refused to consider it. "Crime is such a distressing thing," he had once said, "and it's so implausible to presume that a sane person would voluntarily go beyond the bounds of modesty and virtue, that I'm always extremely reluctant to attribute such things to anyone. We should seldom entertain suspicions of vice; they're often the work of our own vanity, and nearly always the result of a secret comparison that takes place in the depths of our soul: we're eager to admit the possibility of evil in order to be entitled to regard ourselves as better. If we think about it carefully, mustn't we conclude that it's better to leave a real sin undiscovered than to invent imaginary ones because of unforgivable haste, thus dishonoring, in our own eyes, people who have done no wrong other than that which our pride has ascribed to them? And wouldn't everything be better if this principle were always followed? Isn't it much less important to punish a crime than to prevent it from spreading? If we leave it in the darkness it seeks, haven't we, in a sense, destroyed it? A scandal is sure to follow if it's made public, and accounts of it stir up the passions of those who are inclined to the same kind of crime. The inevitable blindness of evil flatters the potential criminal's hope of being more fortunate than the one who has just been discovered. He hasn't been given a lesson, but a piece of advice, and he indulges in excesses he might never have dared to commit if it hadn't been for that imprudent publicity which is falsely regarded as justice, but which is actually nothing but ill-advised severity or disguised vanity."

And so the only decision reached during this first conference was to make a careful investigation of Franval's reasons for not wanting Eugénie to get married, and of her reasons for sharing his views. It was agreed that no action would be undertaken until this information had been acquired.

"Well, Eugénie," Franval said to her that evening, "you've seen for yourself that they want to separate us. Will they succeed, my child? Will they succeed in breaking the sweetest bonds of my life?"

"Never! Have no fear, my dearest friend: the bonds you delight in are as precious to me as they are to you. You didn't deceive me when you formed them, you showed me clearly how strongly they conflicted with our moral standards; but, having no qualms about violating such standards, which vary from place to place and therefore can't be sacred, I accepted those bonds without remorse, so don't be afraid that I may break them."

"Alas, who knows? Colunce is younger than I.... He has everything necessary to enchant you.... You mustn't be misled by a passion that has no doubt blinded you. When age and the light of reason have broken the spell, you'll soon begin to have regrets, you'll confide them to me, and I'll never forgive myself for having caused them!"

"No," Eugénie said firmly, "I'm determined to love only you. I'd consider myself the unhappiest woman in the world if I had to take a husband. What!" she exclaimed heatedly. "How could I bind myself to a stranger who, unlike you, would not have double reasons for loving me, and whose feelings for me would therefore be, at most, no stronger than his desire? Abandoned and despised by him, what would I become? A prude, a religious fanatic, or a prostitute? No, no, I'd rather be your mistress. Yes, I love you a hundred times more than being reduced to playing any of those infamous parts.... But what's the cause of all this commotion?" she asked bitterly. "Do you know who's behind it? Your wife, it can't be anyone else. Her implacable jealousy. . . . You can be sure of it: that's the sole reason for the disaster that threatens us. Ah, I don't blame her! It's perfectly natural and understandable: she's willing to do anything to keep you. What wouldn't I do if I were in her place and someone were trying to take your heart away from me!"

Franval, deeply moved, kissed his daughter again and again. Encouraged by his criminal caresses to reveal her appalling soul more forcefully, she ventured to tell her father, with unpardonable impudence, that the only way for them to be watched less closely would be to give her mother a lover. This plan amused Franval; but, being much more malicious than his daughter, and wishing to begin gradually preparing her young heart for all the seeds of hatred of his wife that he wanted to sow in it, he replied that this vengeance seemed too sweet to him, and that there were other ways of making a woman unhappy when she irritated her husband.

A few weeks went by, during which Franval and his daughter finally decided on the first plan conceived for the despair of that monster's virtuous wife. He rightly believed that before going on to more shameful acts he should at least try to give his wife a lover. Not only would this provide a basis for all the others, but also, if the attempt were successful, it would force Madame de Franval to concern herself less with the sins of others, since she would have sins of her own that were equally well established. With this plan in mind, Franval carefully considered all the young men he knew, and after serious reflection he decided that only Valmont was capable of serving him.

Valmont was thirty years old; with a charming

face, an alert mind, a great deal of imagination and no principles whatever, he was well suited to the part he was going to be asked to play. Franval invited him to lunch one day, and as they were leaving the table he took him aside and said to him, "My friend, I've always considered you worthy of me. The time has come to prove to me that I'm not mistaken: I demand proof of your feelings . . . but a very unusual kind of proof."

"What is it?" said Valmont. "Explain yourself, my friend, and never doubt my eagerness to be useful to you."

"What do you think of my wife?"

"She's delightful; if you weren't her husband, I'd have become her lover long ago."

"Your self-restraint is very considerate, Valmont, but I'm not grateful to you for it."

"What do you mean?"

"I'm going to surprise you: it's precisely because you like me, and because I'm Madame de Franval's husband, that I want you to become her lover."

"Are you mad?"

"No, but I'm whimsical and capricious; you've known me like that for a long time. I want to make my wife's virtue collapse, and I insist that you be the one to bring it about."

"What foolishness!"

"You're wrong: it's a masterpiece of reason."

"What! Do you really want me to make you a . . ."

"Yes. I demand it of you, in fact, and I'll stop considering you as my friend if you refuse me that favor. I'll help you, I'll arrange for you to be alone with her often. You'll take advantage of those opportunities, and as soon as I'm certain of my fate I'll throw myself at your feet, if you like, to thank you for your obligingness."

"Franval, you can't pull the wool over my eyes: there's something odd behind this, and I won't do a thing until I know what it is."

"Yes . . . But I think you're a little squeamish; I don't yet feel that you have enough strength of mind to be capable of understanding this. . . . More prejudices . . . You're no doubt chivalrous. . . . You'll tremble like a child when I've told you everything, and then you'll refuse to do anything."

"You think *I'll* tremble? I'm sorry you have such an opinion of me. Let me tell you, my friend, that there's no kind of vice, no matter how perverse, that's capable of alarming my heart for even an instant."

"Valmont, have you ever looked closely at Eugénie?"

"Your daughter?"

"Yes; or my mistress, if you prefer."

"Ah, you scoundrel! Now I understand!"

"This is the first time I've ever seen you show any perception."

"What! Are you really in love with your daughter?"

"Yes, my friend, the same as Lot; I've always had great respect for the Holy Bible, and I've always been convinced that the way to get to heaven is to imitate its heroes! . . . Ah, my friend, Pygmalion's madness no longer surprises me. . . . Don't such weaknesses occur everywhere? Wasn't it necessary to begin that way in order to populate the world? And if it wasn't wrong then, why should it be wrong now? What nonsense! Is it reasonable to think that I can't be tempted by a pretty girl simply because I brought her into the world? Must I be repelled by the very fact that ought to unite me more intimately with her? Because she resembles me, because she sprang from my blood, in other words, because she combines all the elements capable of producing the most ardent love, must I look on her coldly? Ah, what sophistry! What absurdity! Let fools observe those ridiculous prohibitions, they're meaningless to souls like ours. The dominion of beauty and the holy rights of love are oblivious to trivial human conventions; their power sweeps them away like the morning sun purifying the earth of the mists that cover it during the night. Let us trample those repulsive prejudices under foot; they're always enemies of happiness, and while they may sometimes have led reason astray, it has always been at the expense of the sweetest pleasures. They should be forever despised by us."

"You've convinced me," replied Valmont, "and I'll readily grant that your Eugénie must be a delightful mistress. Her beauty is much livelier than her mother's, and if she doesn't have, as your wife does, that languor which seizes the soul with such voluptuous pleasure, she has that piquancy which subdues us and seems to subjugate anyone who would like to put up any resistance. While one seems to yield, the other demands; what one permits, the other offers, and I find much more charm in the latter."

"But it's not Eugénie I'm giving you, it's her mother."

"What's your reason for doing this?"

"My wife is jealous; she hinders me, she's always watching me. She wants to arrange a marriage for Eugénie. I want to make her commit a sin so that I can cover up my own, and that's why you must have her. You'll amuse yourself with her for a time, and then you'll betray her. I'll catch her in your arms and either punish her or use my discovery to make her let me pursue my errors in peace while I do the same for her. . . . But don't fall in love, Valmont: keep your self-control. Captivate her and don't let her dominate you."

"Have no fear: she'd be the first woman who ever stirred my heart."

Our two scoundrels agreed on their arrangements; it was decided that within a few days Valmont would begin trying to seduce Madame de Franval, with full permission to employ any means to succeed, even a revelation of Franval's amorous intrigue, since it was felt that this would be the most effective way to make that virtuous woman resolve to take vengeance.

Eugénie was greatly amused by the plan when it was described to her; the infamous creature dared to say that if Valmont succeeded, to make her happiness as complete as possible she would have to verify her mother's downfall with her own eyes and see that heroine of virtue yielding incontestably to the charms of a pleasure which she condemned so severely.

Finally the day arrived when the unhappiest and most honorable of women was to receive not only the most painful blow that could have been dealt to her, but also the insult of being abandoned by her horrible husband to the man by whom he had consented to be dishonored. What madness! What contempt of all principles! For what purpose does nature create hearts as depraved as those?

A few preliminary conversations had prepared the scene. Valmont was on such close terms with Franval that his wife could not have suspected that there was any risk in being left alone with him, as had already happened several times before. The three of them were in the drawing room. Franval stood up and said, "I must hurry off to attend to an important matter. Valmont is such an upright man that leaving you with him, madame, is like leaving you with your governess," he added, laughing. "But let me know if he forgets himself: I don't yet like him enough to yield my rights to him. . . ." And the insolent wretch departed.

After a few commonplace remarks based on Franval's jest, Valmont said that for the past six months he had noticed a change in his friend. "I haven't dared to question him about it," he said, "but he seems to have some sort of sorrow."

"One thing is certain," replied Madame de Franval: "he gives plenty of sorrow to others."

"Good heavens! What are you saying? Has my friend been treating you badly?"

"I wish it were still only that!"

"Please tell me; you know my zeal, my unshakable attachment . . ."

"A series of horrible disorders, moral corruption, wrongs of every kind . . . Would you believe it? A highly advantageous marriage was offered to his daughter and he wouldn't even consider it."

At this point the adroit Valmont turned his eyes away with the expression of a man who has begun to understand something, groans inwardly and is afraid to explain himself.

"Aren't you at all surprised by what I've told you, monsieur?" asked Madame de Franval. "Your silence is strange."

"Ah, madame, isn't it better to remain silent than to speak words that will bring despair to those we love?"

"What sort of a riddle is that? Please explain it."

"How can you expect me not to shudder at the thought of opening your eyes?" said Valmont, warmly seizing one of her hands.

"Oh, monsieur!" she said with great animation. "I demand that you either explain yourself or stop speaking altogether. You've placed me in a terrible situation."

"It may be less terrible than the state to which you've reduced me," said Valmont, casting a glance aflame with love at the woman he was trying to seduce.

"What's the meaning of all this, monsieur? You begin by alarming me and making me want an explanation, you dare to say things which I must not and cannot tolerate, and you deprive me of any means of learning from you the secret that's disquieting me so painfully. Speak, monsieur, speak, or you'll drive me to despair."

"Very well, madame, since you demand it, I'll be less obscure, and although it pains me to break your heart, I'll tell you the cruel reason behind your husband's refusal of Monsieur de Colunce's offer. Eugénie . . ."

"Yes?"

"Franval adores her, madame. He's now less her father than her lover, and he would rather die than give her up."

On hearing this fateful revelation, Madame de Franval was so overwhelmed that she fainted. Valmont hurried to her assistance, and as soon as he had revived her he said, "Now you know the cost of the disclosure you demanded of me, madame. I'd give anything if . . ."

"Leave me, monsieur, leave me," said Madame de Franval, in a state that would be difficult to describe, after such a violent shock. "I need to be alone for a time. . . ."

"You want me to leave you in this situation? Ah, my soul feels your grief so keenly that I can't help asking you to let me share it! I've made the wound, allow me to heal it."

"Franval is in love with his daughter! Good heavens! I carried that creature in my womb, and now she's tearing my heart out! Oh, monsieur, how can it be? Are you quite certain?"

"If I still had any doubt, madame, I would have remained silent; I would far rather have said nothing, to avoid the risk of alarming you in vain. It was from your husband himself that I learned of that infamy. He confided in me . . . In any case, please be calm. Let's now turn our attention to the means of breaking off that intrigue, rather than those of bringing it to light. Those means depend on you alone. . . ."

"Ah, tell me quickly what they are! I'm horrified by that crime."

"Madame, a husband with Franval's character can't be brought back by virtue. He doesn't believe in the virtue of women; he says it's only the fruit of their pride or their temperament, and that what they do to preserve themselves for us is done more to content themselves than to please or attract us. . . . Forgive me, madame, but I won't conceal from you that I'm more or less in agreement with him on the subject; I've never seen a wife succeed in destroying her husband's vices by using virtue. Franval would be much more strongly affected by conduct similar to his own, and you would be much more likely to win him back. Jealousy would be the inevitable result, and so many hearts have been restored to love by that always infallible means! When your husband sees that the virtue to which he has become accustomed, and which he has been insolent enough to despise, is much more the work of reflection than of unconcern or the physical organs, he will learn to respect it in you, at the very moment when he believes you capable of casting it aside. . . . He thinks . . . he dares to say that if you've never had a lover, it's only because you've never been attacked. Prove to him that you can be attacked whenever you choose, that you can take vengeance on him for his mistreatment and contempt. Perhaps you'll have done a little wrong, according to your strict principles, but think of all the wrong you'll have prevented! Think of the husband you'll have converted! For a slight outrage against the goddess you hold in reverence, you'll have brought a disciple back into her temple. Madame, I appeal only to your reason. By the conduct I venture to prescribe to you, you will win Franval back permanently, you will captivate him forever. He's already moving away from you; if you maintain your present line of conduct, he'll escape from you altogether and never return. Yes, madame, I dare to affirm that if you hesitate for an instant, you do not love your husband."

Madame de Franval, greatly surprised by these words, remained for some time without answering. Then, recalling Valmont's earlier remarks and the way he had looked at her, she said artfully, "Monsieur, supposing I were to follow your advice, whom do you think I ought to choose in order to upset my husband most?"

"Ah, my dear and divine friend!" cried Valmont, not seeing the trap that had been set for him. "You ought to choose the one man in the world who loves you more than any other, the man who has adored you ever since he came to know you, and who swears at your feet to die under your dominion . . ."

"Leave, monsieur," Madame de Franval said imperiously, "and never appear before my eyes again. Your ruse has been uncovered: to further your treacherous scheme of seduction, you've accused my husband of a crime he's incapable of committing. And even if he were guilty, the means you've offered me is so repugnant to my heart that I would never dream of employing it. A husband's failings never justify those of a wife; she ought to regard them as only one more reason for being virtuous, so that the righteous man, whom the Almighty will find in the afflicted cities ready to undergo the effects of His anger, may ward off the flames that are about to consume them."

With these words, Madame de Franval walked out of the room. She sent for Valmont's servants and forced him to leave, very much ashamed of the beginning he had just made.

Although that attractive woman had seen through Valmont's guile, what he had said corresponded so closely to what she and her mother feared that she resolved to do everything in her power to investigate those cruel facts. She went to see her mother, told her what had happened, and came back after having decided on the steps we are about to see her take.

It was said long ago, and quite rightly, that we have no greater enemies than our own servants. Always jealous and envious, they seem to try to lighten their chains by exposing shortcomings which place us beneath them and therefore gratify their vanity, for a short time at least, with the superiority over us which fate has denied them.

Madame de Franval bribed one of Eugénie's maids. This creature was swayed by the promise of security and a happy life, and by the appearance of doing a good deed. She agreed to enable Madame de Franval to dispel all doubts of her misfortune the following night.

The time came. The unhappy mother was admitted into a room adjoining the one in which her faithless husband nightly insulted heaven and desecrated his marriage. Eugénie was with her father. Several candles were burning on a corner cupboard, ready to illuminate the crime. The altar was prepared; the victim took her place on it, the sacrificer followed her. . . . Madame de Franval was sustained only by her despair, her outraged love and her courage. She burst open the doors that restrained her and rushed into the room. She fell to her knees, weeping, at the feet of the incestuous Franval and cried out to him: "O you who fill my life with sorrow, I haven't deserved such treatment from you! I still adore you, no matter how great the wrongs you've inflicted on me. See my tears . . . and don't spurn me. I beg you to have mercy on this poor girl who, deceived by her weakness and your seduction, thinks she can find happiness in shamelessness and crime. . . . Eugénie, Eugénie, do you want to cause the death of the woman who gave you life? Stop being the accomplice of the atrocious crime whose horror is being concealed from you! Come to me, come! See my arms ready to receive you! See your heartbroken mother at your feet, begging you not to outrage honor and nature . . . But if you both refuse me," continued that disconsolate woman, holding a dagger to her heart, "this is the means I'll use to escape the dishonor you're trying to cast on me. I'll stain you both with my blood, and you'll have to consummate your crime over my sad body."

That Franval's hardened soul was able to resist that spectacle is a fact which will be easily believed by those who are beginning to know that scoundrel, but that Eugénie was also unmoved by it is something which surpasses all understanding.

"Madame," said that corrupted girl with cruel calm, "I confess that I find it difficult to believe in your rationality after the ridiculous scene you've just made in your husband's bedroom. Isn't he free to do as he pleases? And if he approves of my conduct, what right have you to condemn it? Do we pry into your peccadilloes with Monsieur de Valmont? Do we disturb you in your pleasures? Please respect ours, or else don't be surprised if I urge your husband to take steps that will force you to do so . . ."

At this moment Madame de Franval lost patience entirely and all her anger turned against the ignoble creature who had so thoroughly forgotten herself as to speak to her that way. She furiously stood up and leapt toward her, but the cruel and odious Franval seized his wife by the hair and, in a rage, pulled her away from his daughter and dragged her out of the room. He threw her violently down the stairs; she fell, bleeding and unconscious, before the door of one of her maids. Having been awakened by the terrible noise, the maid quickly saved her mistress from the fury of her tyrant, who was already coming down the stairs to finish off his hapless victim. After locking the door of her room she began treating Madame de Franval's injuries, while the monster who had just attacked her so savagely hurried back to his detestable paramour to spend the night as peacefully as if he had not reduced himself below the level of the most ferocious beast by assaults so execrable, so debasing, so horrible, in a word, that we blush at having to reveal them.

Poor Madame de Franval no longer had any of her illusions left, and there were no others that she could adopt. It was all too clear that her husband's heart, the heart that was the dearest of all to her, had been taken away from her. And by whom? By the girl who owed her more respect than anyone else, and who had just spoken to her with such insolence. She had also surmised that the whole situation with Valmont was nothing but a vile trap whose purpose was to make her guilty if possible, or, if not, to accuse her of guilt, to cover her with it in order to counterbalance and justify the infinitely more serious wrong that was being done to her.

Nothing could have been more accurate. On learning of Valmont's failure, Franval had instructed him to replace reality with imposture and indiscretion, to circulate the story that he was Madame de Franval's lover; and it was decided that they would have a forger produce abominable letters that would constitute unequivocal evidence of the adulterous affair in which Franval's unfortunate wife had refused to become involved.

Meanwhile, in despair and even injured in several parts of her body, Madame de Franval fell seriously ill. Her barbarous husband, refusing to see her and not even deigning to inquire about her condition, left for the country with Eugénie, on the pretext that there was fever in the house and he did not want to expose her to it.

Valmont presented himself several times at Madame de Franval's door during her illness, but she never received him. Except for her loving mother and Monsieur de Clervil, she saw no one at all. Comforted by these dear friends, who were so worthy of having rights over her, and revived by their care, at the end of forty days she was able to have visitors. Franval then brought Eugénie back to Paris and they made preparations with Valmont to provide themselves with weapons capable of counteracting those which Madame de Franval and her friends were apparently going to use against them.

Our scoundrel went to see his wife as soon as he thought she was well enough to receive him.

"Madame," he said to her coldly, "you're surely aware of my interest in your condition; I can't conceal from you the fact that it's the sole cause of Eugénie's self-restraint: she had decided to lodge a vigorous complaint against you for the way you treated her. However firmly convinced she may be of the respect a daughter owes to her mother, she can't fail to recognize that a mother places herself in an extremely bad position if she lunges at her daughter with a dagger in her hand. An impulsive act like that, madame, might open the eyes of the government to your conduct and eventually destroy your freedom as well as your honor."

"I wasn't expecting such recriminations, monsieur," replied Madame de Franval, "after my daughter, seduced by you, has made herself guilty of incest, adultery, licentiousness and odious ingratitude toward the woman who brought her into the world. . . . Yes, I confess that, after that complex web of horrors, I didn't think it would be I who might have to fear a complaint. It takes someone with all your cunning and malice, monsieur, to accuse innocence while excusing crime so audaciously!"

"I realize, madame, that the odious suspicions you've dared to form with regard to me were the pretext for your scene, but delusions do not justify crime. What you've thought is false; what you've done is unfortunately all too real. You express surprise at the reproaches my daughter addressed to you concerning your affair with Valmont, and yet she discovered the disorders of your conduct long after everyone else in Paris. Your intrigue is so well known, and the proofs of it are unfortunately so solid, that those who mention it to you are guilty at most of indiscretion, but not of calumny."

"*I*, monsieur?" said that virtuous wife, standing up indignantly. "*I* have an affair with Valmont? Good heavens! It's you who've said it!" Tears streamed down her cheeks. "Ingrate! That's how you appreciate my tenderness! That's my reward for having loved you so much! You're not satisfied with outraging me so cruelly, it's not enough for you to have seduced my own daughter: you also have to try to justify your crimes by accusing me of one that would be more horrible than death to me. . . ." She recovered her composure. "You say you have proofs of that intrigue, monsieur. Let me see them; I demand that they be made public, and I'll force you to show them to everyone if you refuse to let me see them."

"No, madame, I won't show them to everyone; it's not usually a husband who makes such things public; he grieves over them, and does his best to hide them. But if you demand them for yourself, madame, I certainly won't refuse them to you. . . ." He took a letter-case from his pocket and said, "Please sit down; you must verify this calmly. Ill-humor and anger would only be detrimental without convincing me, so please control yourself, and let's discuss this soberly."

Madame de Franval, thoroughly convinced of her innocence, did not know what to think of these preparations, and her surprise, mingled with her fear, placed her in a violent state.

"First of all, madame," said Franval, emptying one side of the letter-case, "here's your entire correspondence with Valmont for the past six months. Don't accuse him of imprudence or indiscretion: he's no doubt too upright to treat you with such disrespect. But one of his servants, more adroit than his master is attentive, managed to get me this precious evidence of your extreme purity and your outstanding virtue." He leafed through the letters he had spread out on the table. "Allow me to select, from among these commonplace letters of a woman overheated by a very attractive man, one which seemed to me even more dissolute and more decisive than the others. Here it is, madame:

'My boring husband is having supper this evening in his little house on the outskirts of the city with that horrible creature whom I can't believe I really brought into the world. Come, my dear, and console me for all the sorrows those two monsters give me. But what am I saying? Isn't it the greatest service they could render me now? Doesn't that affair prevent my husband from becoming aware of ours? Let him pursue it as ardently as he wishes, but let him not try to break the bonds that attach me to the only man in the world I have ever really adored.'

"Well, madame?"

"Well, monsieur, I admire you," replied Madame de Franval. "Each day adds to the amazing esteem you so richly deserve. And despite all the great abilities I recognized in you before, I must confess that I didn't know you were also gifted for forgery and calumny."

"Then you deny the evidence?"

"Not at all, I ask only to be convinced. We'll have judges appointed, and experts, and, if you're willing, we'll ask that severe punishment be given to whichever of us proves to be guilty."

"Now there's real effrontery! Good, I like that better than sorrow! Let's continue . . ." He shook out the other part of the letter-case. "There's nothing extraordinary, madame, about the fact that you have a 'boring husband' and a lover with a handsome face. But allow me to find it a little less inconsequential that, at your age, you should be supporting your lover at my expense. Here are accounts totaling over three hundred thousand livres, which you've either paid or agreed in your own handwriting to pay for Valmont. Please examine them," added that monster, showing them to her without letting her touch them. "Here's one from Zaïde, the jeweler: 'I hereby agree to pay the sum of twenty-two thousand livres on the account of Monsieur de Valmont, by arrangement with him. Farneille de Franval.' Here's one for six thousand livres from Jamet, the horse merchant. . . . It was for that team of dark bay horses which are now Valmont's delight and are admired by everyone in Paris. . . . Yes, madame, the grand total is three hundred thousand two hundred eighty-three livres and ten sous; you still owe a third of it, and you've honorably paid the rest. . . . Well, madame?"

"Ah, monsieur, this fraud is too crude to cause me the slightest concern. I demand only one thing to vanquish those who've perpetrated it: let the people for whom I'm alleged to have signed these documents come forward and swear that I've had dealings with them."

"They will, madame, don't doubt it. Would they have told me about your conduct themselves if they weren't prepared to back up what they've said? If it hadn't been for me, in fact, one of them would have had a writ issued against you today. . . ."

Bitter tears welled up in the beautiful eyes of that unhappy woman. Her courage ceased to sustain her; she fell into a fit of despair, accompanied by alarming symptoms: she struck her head against the marble objects that surrounded her, and scratched her face.

"Monsieur," she cried, throwing herself at her husband's feet, "please do away with me by less slow and horrible means! Since my existence hinders you, eliminate it with one blow, don't push me into my grave so slowly. . . . Am I guilty of having loved you, of having rebelled against what was so cruelly taking your heart away from me? If so, punish me, barbarian! Yes, plunge this steel into my bosom without pity," she said, reaching for his sword, "but at least let me die worthy of your esteem, let me take with me into the grave, as my only consolation, the certainty that you believe me to be incapable of the infamous acts you've attributed to me only in order to cover up your own. . . ."

She was on her knees before him. Her head was thrown back, her hands were bleeding, wounded by the bare blade she was trying to seize and thrust into her bosom; that lovely bosom was uncovered, her hair hung down over it in disorder, wet with the tears that she was shedding abundantly. Never had grief been more deeply moving or expressive, never had it been seen in a nobler, more touching or more appealing guise.

"No, madame," said Franval, resisting her movement, "It's not your death that's desired, but your punishment. I understand your repentance, your tears don't surprise me: you're furious at having been discovered. I'm glad to see that attitude in you. It makes me feel that you're going to mend your ways, and you'll no doubt be pushed still faster in that direction by the fate I have in store for you. I'm going off to give it my attention now."

"Stop, Franval!" cried his unhappy wife. "Don't spread the news of your dishonor, don't make it common knowledge that you're guilty of perjury, forgery, incest and calumny. . . . Since you want to be rid of me, I'll leave you, I'll find a refuge where even your memory will fade from my mind. You'll be free, you can be a criminal with impunity. Yes, I'll forget you . . . if I can, cruel man. But if your painful image doesn't leave my heart, if it still pursues me in my deep obscurity, I won't obliterate it, traitor: that effort would be beyond my strength; no, I won't obliterate it, but I'll punish myself for my blindness, and I'll bury in the horror of the grave the sinful altar on which you were cherished too much. . . ."

With these words, the last outburst of a soul cast down by a recent illness, she fell unconscious to the floor. The cold shadows of death spread over the roses of her beautiful complexion, roses that had already been withered by despair. She was little more than a lifeless mass, yet she was still not abandoned by her grace, her modesty, and all the other charms of virtue. The monster left her and went to enjoy with his sinful daughter the frightful triumph which vice, or rather iniquity, had dared to win over innocence and misfortune.

Franval's execrable daughter was greatly pleased by these details. She wished she could have seen them. She also wished that horror could be carried still further, that Valmont could triumph over her mother's severity, and that Franval could catch them together. If that happened, what means of justification would be left to their victim? And was it not important to make sure she had none? Such was Eugénie.

Meanwhile, since Franval's poor wife had only her mother's bosom on which to weep, it was not long before she told her of her new reasons for sorrow. It was then that it occurred to Madame de Farneille that Monsieur de Clervil's age, calling and prestige might have some effect on her son-in-law. Nothing is as confident as unhappiness. She informed the respectable clergyman of Franval's disorders as well as she could. She convinced him of what he had never been willing to believe, and urged him to employ with such a scoundrel only that persuasive eloquence which appeals to the heart rather than to the mind. Then she suggested that after he had talked with Franval he should have a conversation with Eugénie during which he would use every means he thought best to open her eyes to the abyss that was opening beneath her feet, and to bring her back, if possible, to her mother and to virtue.

Franval, informed that Clervil was going to ask to see him and his daughter, had time to work out a plan with her. When they had done this, they sent word to Madame de Farneille's confessor that they were ready to hear him. The credulous Madame de Franval placed great hopes in the eloquence of her spiritual guide. Those who are unhappy clutch at shadows, and, to give themselves an enjoyment that truth refuses to them, they artfully bring into being all sorts of illusions.

Clervil arrived at nine o'clock in the morning. Franval received him in the room where he usually spent his nights with his daughter; he had had it embellished with all possible elegance, yet at the same time he had allowed it to retain a kind of disorder which gave evidence of his criminal pleasures. . . . Eugénie was in an adjoining room from which she could hear everything, so that she would be better able to prepare herself for the conversation she was going to have in her turn.

"I've come to you in great fear of disturbing you, monsieur," said Clervil. "Men of my calling are usually so burdensome to people who, like you, devote all their time to the pleasures of this world, that I reproach myself for having yielded to Madame de Farneille's wishes by asking you to allow me to speak with you for a few moments."

"Sit down, monsieur; and as long as the language of justice and reason reigns in what you say, you need have no fear of boring me."

"Monsieur, you're adored by a young wife, full of charms and virtues, whom you're accused of making very unhappy. Having nothing on her side except her innocence and candor, having only her mother to listen to her complaints, still idolizing you despite the wrong you've done her, she's in a terrible position, as you can easily imagine."

"I'd like to come to the point, monsieur. What is the object of your visit?"

"To bring you back to happiness, if possible."

"In that case, if I'm happy the way I am, you have nothing more to say to me."

"It's impossible, monsieur, for happiness to be found in crime."

"I agree. But a man who, by profound study and mature reflection, has been able to bring his mind to the point where he suspects evil in nothing, and sees all human acts with tranquil indifference and considers them all as the necessary results of a Power, whatever its nature, which, sometimes good and sometimes perverse, but always imperious, inspires us alternately with what men approve and what they condemn, but never with anything that disturbs it—such a man, you will agree, monsieur, can be as happy in living a life like mine as in pursuing the career you've chosen. Happiness is ideal, it's the work of the imagination. It's a way of being moved which depends solely on our way of seeing and feeling. Except for the satisfaction of needs, there's nothing that makes all men equally happy. Every day we see one man made happy by something that's extremely displeasing to another. Consequently there is no certain happiness, and there can be none for us except that which we form with the aid of our organs and our principles."

"I know that, monsieur, but while our mind may deceive us, our conscience never leads us astray: it's the book in which nature has written all our duties."

"But don't we do whatever we like with that factitious conscience? Habit bends it; it's like a piece of soft wax that takes on all shapes beneath our fingers. If that book were as sure as you say it is, wouldn't man have an invariable conscience? Wouldn't all acts be the same for him, from one end of the earth to the other? But is this the case? Does the Hottentot tremble from what frightens the Frenchman? And doesn't the Frenchman do things every day that would cause him to be punished in Japan? No, monsieur, there's nothing real in the world, nothing that deserves praise or blame, nothing that's worthy of being rewarded or punished, nothing unjust here that may not be lawful a thousand miles away; in short, there's no real evil or unchanging good."

"Don't believe it, monsieur: virtue is not an illusion. It's not necessary to know that something is good here and bad somewhere else in order to give it a precise designation of crime or virtue, and to be certain that one will find happiness or not, depending on the choice one makes. Happiness resides only in complete submission to the laws of one's country. One must either respect them or be miserable; there is no middle ground between breaking them and being unhappy. If we do something that's forbidden, whether it's intrinsically good or bad, we shall experience adverse consequences not from the thing itself, but from its conflict with the social conventions of the locality in which we live. There is certainly no harm in preferring to walk on the boulevards rather than on the Champs Élysées, and yet if a law were promulgated that forbade all citizens to walk on the boulevards, anyone who broke that law might be causing himself an endless chain of misfortunes, even though he had done only a perfectly natural thing in breaking it. Furthermore, the habit of violating ordinary prohibitions soon leads us to violate more serious ones, and, going from one error to another, we finally come to crimes that are punished in every country in the world, and arouse dread in every reasonable person on earth, wherever he may live. If there is no universal conscience for man, there is at least a national one relating to the existence we've received from nature, and in which her hand has written our duties in letters that we cannot erase without danger. For example, monsieur, your family accuses you of incest; no matter what sophisms may have been used to justify that crime and try to lessen its horror, no matter what specious arguments have been applied to it, and no matter how much they have been supported with examples drawn from neighboring countries, it is no less demonstrably true that this crime, which is a crime only among certain peoples, is certainly dangerous where it is forbidden by law. It is also certain that it may give rise to terrible consequences, and other crimes necessitated by the first, crimes which deserve to be held in horror by all men. If you had married your daughter on the banks of the Ganges, where such marriages are permitted, you might have committed only a very minor wrong; but in a country where such unions are forbidden, by offering that revolting picture to the public and to the eyes of a woman who adores you and is being driven to her grave by your treachery, you have without doubt committed a frightful act, a crime which tends to break the holiest bonds of nature, those which attach your daughter to the woman who gave her life and ought to make her regard that woman as the most respectable and sacred person in the world. You're forcing your daughter to despise her most precious duties, you're making her hate the woman who carried her in her womb; and, without realizing it, you're preparing the weapons she may use against you. Your condemnation is engraved on all the ideas you present to her, on all the principles you instill in her; and if some day her hand makes an attempt on your life, you yourself will have sharpened the dagger."

"Your way of reasoning, so different from that of most men of your calling, monsieur," replied Franval, "obliges me to have confidence in you. I could deny your accusation; I hope that my frankness in revealing myself to you will make you believe in my wife's sins when I describe them to you with the same truthfulness that will guide me in confessing my own. Yes, monsieur, I love my daughter, I love her passionately, she's my mistress, my sister, my confidante, my friend, my only divinity on earth; in short, she has every possible claim to the homage of a heart, and I've given her all the homage of mine. These feelings will last as long as my life. Since I'm unable to give them up, I'm no doubt obliged to justify them.

"The first duty of a father toward his daughter is undeniably, as I'm sure you'll agree, monsieur, to procure the greatest possible amount of happiness for her. If he has not done this, he has failed in his obligations to her; if he has done it, he is secure from all reproach. I've neither forced nor misled Eugénie—that's a noteworthy fact, don't let it escape you. I've never hidden the world from her. I described the roses of marriage to her, along with the thorns that are found in it. I then offered myself and left her free to choose. She didn't hesitate: she said that she could find happiness only with me. Was I wrong to give her, for her own happiness, what she seemed to prefer, with full knowledge, to everything else?"

"Those sophisms justify nothing, monsieur. You shouldn't have given your daughter the idea that the man she could not prefer without crime could become the object of her happiness. No matter how beautiful a fruit might appear, wouldn't you regret offering it to someone if you were sure that death was hidden within it? No, monsieur, no, you've considered only yourself in your unfortunate conduct, and you've made your daughter both its accomplice and its victim. What you've done is unforgivable. . . . And what wrong do you attribute to that virtuous and sensitive wife whose heart you're callously breaking? What wrong has she done, unjust man, except that of idolizing you?"

"That's what I want to discuss with you, monsieur, and it's now that I hope you'll show confidence in me. I think I have some right to expect it, after the frankness with which I've admitted the truth of the accusation against me."

Franval showed Clervil the false letters and accounts he had imputed to his wife, and certified their reality and that of her affair with Valmont. Clervil knew everything.

"Well, monsieur," he said firmly to Franval, "wasn't I right to say that an error which seems inconsequential at first may, by accustoming us to going beyond limits, lead us into the utmost excesses of crime and wickedness? You began with an act which you considered trivial, but now you can see all the infamous things you've had to do to justify or conceal it. . . . Take my advice, monsieur: throw those unpardonable atrocities into the fire, and let's forget them entirely."

"These documents are genuine, monsieur."

"They're false."

"You can only be in doubt; is that enough for you to contradict me?"

"Excuse me, monsieur, but I have no reason to consider them genuine except what you've said, and you have a great interest in supporting your accusation. To consider them false, I have your wife's word, and she, too, would have a great interest in telling me they were genuine, if they were. That's how I judge, monsieur: self-interest is the guide to all human actions, and wherever I find it I immediately see the light of truth. I've been following that rule for forty years and it hasn't failed me yet. . . . Besides, your wife's virtue will destroy your abominable calumny in everyone's eyes. With her guileless, candid nature, and with the love for you that still burns in her heart, is it plausible that she should commit such abominations? No, that's not how crime begins; since you know its effects so well, you should have contrived it more cleverly."

"You're insulting me, monsieur!"

"Forgive me; injustice, calumny and licentiousness shock my soul so profoundly that I'm sometimes unable to control the agitation into which those horrors plunge me. Let's burn those papers, monsieur, I beg you. . . . Let's burn them for the sake of your honor and your peace of mind."

"I didn't think, monsieur," said Franval, standing up, "that in your calling one became so easily the apologist and protector of misconduct and adultery.

My wife is disgracing me and ruining me, and I've proved it to you, but your blindness with regard to her makes you prefer to accuse me and look on me as a slanderer, rather than consider her a faithless and debauched woman! Well, monsieur, the law will decide. Every court in France will resound with my complaints. I'll present my proofs, I'll make my dishonor public, and then we'll see whether you'll still be so guileless, or rather so foolish, as to protect such a shameless creature against me."

"I'll leave you now, monsieur," said Clervil, also standing up. "I didn't think that the faults of your mind had so greatly deteriorated the qualities of your heart, and that, blinded by an unjust desire for vengeance, you had become capable of cool-headedly maintaining things which could only have been born of delirium. . . . All this has convinced me more firmly than ever that when a man has violated his most sacred duty, he soon allows himself to trample on all the others. . . . If your reflections should make you change your mind, please let me know, and in your family and me you will always find friends who are ready to receive you. . . . Would you allow me to see your daughter for a few moments?"

"As you wish, monsieur. And let me urge you to use sounder or more eloquent arguments in presenting to her those luminous truths in which I was unfortunate enough to see only blindness and sophistry."

Clervil went into Eugénie's room. She was waiting for him in an elegant and attractive negligee. This kind of indecency, the fruit of crime and self-abandon, reigned impudently in her gestures and her gaze. Insulting the physical charms that made her beautiful in spite of her character, the unscrupulous girl combined all the qualities that excite vice and offend virtue.

Since it would not have been suitable for a young girl to enter into details as profoundly as a philosopher like Franval, Eugénie limited herself to malicious banter. Her conduct gradually became strongly provocative, but she soon saw that her seductive efforts were wasted, and that a man as virtuous as the one with whom she was dealing would not allow himself to be caught in her trap. She deftly loosened the knots that held the veil of her charms, and thus placed herself in a state of great disorder before Clervil had time to notice.

"The wretch!" she cried loudly. "Take this monster away from me! And make sure my father doesn't learn of his crime! Good heavens! I was expecting pious advice from him, and the vile man attacked my modesty. . . . Look," she said to the servants who had hurried into the room on hearing her cries, "look at the state this insolent man has put me in! That's how they behave, those benevolent votaries of a divinity that they outrage! Scandal, debauchery, seduction—that's what their morals are composed of, and, taken in by their false virtue, we're foolish enough to revere them!"

Although he was greatly irritated by this scene, Clervil succeeded in hiding his emotion. As he walked away with composure, through the crowd that had surrounded him, he said calmly, "May heaven preserve that unfortunate girl. May it make her better if it can, and may no one in this house offend her feelings of virtue more than I have done. I came not to defile them, but to try to revive them in her heart."

Such were the only results of the mission from which Madame de Farneille and her daughter had expected so much. They were far from knowing the degradations that crime produces in the souls of the wicked; they are only embittered by what would have a salutary effect on others, and it is in the very lessons of good that they find encouragements to evil.

From then on, things became more venomous on both sides. Franval and Eugénie saw that they would have to convince Madame de Franval of her supposed sins in a way that would leave her no doubt, and Madame de Farneille, in concert with her daughter, began making serious plans to abduct Eugénie. They spoke to Clervil about these plans. Their upright friend refused to take part in such a drastic course of action. He said that he had been too badly mistreated in that affair to be able to do anything but implore forgiveness for the two culprits; he prayed for it earnestly, and steadfastly refused to perform any other kind of service or mediation. What sublimity of sentiments! Why is such nobility so rare among men of his calling? Or why had that unique man adopted a calling so tainted with dishonor?

Let us begin with Franval's undertakings.

Valmont returned.

"You're an imbecile," said Eugénie's sinful lover, "you're unworthy of being my pupil, and I'll spread your disgrace all over Paris if you don't behave better with my wife the next time you see her. You must have her, my friend, you must genuinely have her, so that I can see her defeat with my own eyes. I must be able to deprive that detestable creature of all means of excuse and defense."

"But what if she resists?" said Valmont.

"You'll use violence. I'll make sure that no one is nearby. Frighten her, threaten her, what does it matter?

I'll regard all the means of your triumph as so many outstanding services on your part."

"Listen," said Valmont, "I consent to what you're proposing, I give you my word that your wife will yield, but I demand one condition, and I won't do anything if you refuse. As you know, jealousy must play no part in our arrangements. I demand that you let me spend a quarter of an hour alone with Eugénie. You can't imagine how I'll act when I've enjoyed the pleasure of talking with her a little while."

"But, Valmont . . ."

"I understand your fears, but if you think I'm your friend, I won't forgive you for them: I want only the delights of seeing Eugénie alone, and of talking with her for a few moments."

"Valmont," said Franval, somewhat surprised, "You attach much too high a price to your services. I know all the ridiculous aspects of jealousy as well as you do, but I idolize Eugénie and I'd rather give up my fortune than cede her favors."

"I don't aspire to them, so put your mind at rest."

Realizing that no one else among his acquaintances was capable of serving him as well as Valmont, Franval was eager not to let him escape from him.

"Well, I repeat that your services are costly," he said, rather irritably. "In giving them to me this way, you dispense me from being grateful."

"Gratitude is only the reward of honest services: it will never be kindled in your heart for those I'm going to render you. In fact, they'll turn us against each other within two months. I know how men are, my friend, I know their faults and failings and everything they involve. Place the human animal, the most vicious of all, in any situation you please, and I'll predict all the results that will follow. . . . I want to be paid in advance, or I won't do anything."

"I accept," said Franval.

"Very well, then," replied Valmont, "everything depends on your wishes now. I'll act whenever you say."

"I'll need some time to make my preparations, but within four days, at the most, I'll be ready."

After the upbringing he had given his daughter, Franval was quite sure that no excess of modesty would make her refuse to take part in the plans he had worked out with Valmont. But he was jealous, and Eugénie knew it. She loved him at least as much as he loved her, and as soon as he told her what had been decided she confessed to him that she was very much afraid that her private conversation with Valmont might have undesirable consequences. Franval thought he knew Valmont well enough to be sure that all this would only nourish his mind without presenting any danger to his heart; he dispelled Eugénie's fears as well as he could, and all his preparations were made.

It was then that Franval was informed by some servants in his mother-in-law's house, who were secretly in his pay and in whom he had complete confidence, that Eugénie was in great peril, because Madame de Farneille was about to obtain an order to have her taken away. Franval had no doubt that the plot was Clervil's work. He temporarily set aside his plans with Valmont and turned all his attention to getting rid of the unfortunate clergyman whom he so falsely believed to be the instigator of everything. He distributed money lavishly; this powerful servant of all the vices was placed in many different hands, and finally he had six reliable scoundrels ready to carry out his orders.

One evening when Clervil, who often had supper with Madame de Farneille, was leaving her house alone and on foot, he was surrounded, seized, told that he was being arrested by the government, and shown a counterfeit order. He was then put into a post chaise and taken with all possible speed to the dungeon of an isolated castle which Franval owned in the Ardennes. He was turned over to the porter of this castle as an unscrupulous man who had tried to kill his master, and the best precautions were taken to prevent that unfortunate victim, whose only crime was having been too indulgent to those who were outraging him so cruelly, from ever reappearing in the light of day.

Madame de Farneille was in despair. She had no doubt that her son-in-law was responsible for Clervil's disappearance. Her efforts to find him slowed her preparations for Eugénie's abduction. With few acquaintances and very little influence, it was difficult to deal with two such important undertakings at once; and furthermore, Franval's vigorous action had alarmed Madame de Farneille and her daughter. They thought only of their confessor, but all their attempts to find him were in vain; our reprobate had laid his plans so well that it was impossible to discover anything.

At first Madame de Franval, who had not spoken to her husband since their last scene, was afraid to question him. But a powerful interest overrides all other considerations, and she finally had the courage to ask her tyrant if he intended to add to all his other mistreatment of her by depriving her mother of the best friend she had in the world. The monster defended himself; he carried hypocrisy to the point of offering to make investigations of his own. Realizing that he needed to soften her attitude in preparation for Valmont's scene, he promised that he would do everything possible to find Clervil. He caressed his credulous wife and assured her that no matter how unfaithful he might be to her, it was impossible for him not to adore her from the depths of his soul; and Madame de Franval, still gentle and obliging, still glad of anything that brought her closer to the man who was dearer to her than life, lent herself to all his desires, anticipated them, served them, and shared them all, without daring to take advantage of that opportunity, as she should have, to make him promise to improve his conduct, which was plunging her into an abyss of torment and sorrow every day. But would she have been successful if she had tried? Would Franval, so deceitful in all the other acts of his life, have been any more sincere in the one which, according to him, was enjoyable only insofar as one went beyond certain limits? He would no doubt have given her his promise solely for the delight of breaking it; he might even have wanted her to demand an oath of him, so that he could add the spice of perjury to his abominable pleasures.

Franval, absolutely at peace, turned all his thoughts to troubling others. Such was his vindictive, turbulent, impetuous character: when he was disquieted, he wanted to recover his tranquillity at any cost, and to do so he awkwardly employed only those means most likely to make him lose it again. If he regained it, he immediately began using all his mental and physical faculties to do harm. Thus, always in action, he either had to forestall the ruses he forced others to use against him, or else he had to direct ruses of his own against them.

Everything was arranged to Valmont's satisfaction; his private conversation with Eugénie lasted for an hour in her apartment.

"Well, are you content now?" said Franval, rejoining his friend.

"She's a delightful girl," replied Valmont. "But I advise you not to take such a risk with any other man. You can be glad of the sentiments in my heart which protect you from all danger."

"I'm counting on them," Franval said rather seriously. "And now, act as soon as you can."

"I'll prepare your wife tomorrow. As you can well understand, I'll need a preliminary conversation. Four days later, you can be sure of me."

They exchanged promises and parted.

But after his conversation with Eugénie, Valmont had no desire to betray Madame de Franval or to make his friend more secure in a conquest of which he had become too envious. Eugénie had made such a deep impression on him that he could not tolerate the idea of being without her. He was determined at all costs to have her as his wife. On thinking about it calmly, once he was no longer repelled by her affair with her father, he reflected that his fortune was as great as Colunce's, that he was equally entitled to ask for her hand, and that he could not be refused. He felt that by making zealous efforts to break Eugénie's incestuous bonds, and by promising her family to succeed, he would be sure to obtain the object of his devotion. He would no doubt have to fight a duel with Franval, but his courage and skill made him confident of its outcome.

These reflections took place within twenty-four hours, and Valmont's mind was still full of them when he went to see Madame de Franval. She had been informed of his visit in advance. It will be recalled that during her last meeting with her husband she had almost become reconciled with him; having yielded to his insidious wiles, she could no longer refuse to see Valmont. She had objected, citing the letters and documents he had shown her, and the ideas he had expressed; but he had assured her with apparent unconcern that the surest way of convincing others that her affair with Valmont was imaginary, or had ceased to exist, would be to see him the same as ever, that she would be lending support to suspicion if she refused to do so, and that the best proof a woman could give of her innocence was to go on publicly seeing the man with whom her name had been linked by gossip. This reasoning was sophistical, and Madame de Franval was clearly aware of it, but she hoped to obtain an explanation from Valmont, and her desire to have it, combined with her desire not to anger her husband, had blinded her to the reasons that should have prevented her from seeing the young man. As soon as Valmont arrived, Franval hurried away, leaving them alone together as he had done the last time; he wanted the conversation to be animated and long. Filled with his ideas, Valmont shortened the preliminaries and came straight to the point.

"Oh, madame, don't look on me as the same man who made himself so guilty in your eyes the last time he saw you!" he hastened to say. "I was then the accomplice of your husband's wrongs; I now hope to undo them. Trust me, madame, please accept my word of honor that I haven't come here to lie to you or mislead you in any way."

He then acknowledged the forged letters and documents and apologized profusely for having associated himself with them. He warned Madame de Franval of the new horrors that were being demanded of him. To establish his frankness, he admitted his feelings for Eugénie, revealed what had been done, and promised to break off everything, to abduct Eugénie and take her to one of Madame de Farneille's estates in Picardy, if both ladies would give him their permission and agree to reward him by allowing him to marry the girl he had saved from the abyss.

These statements and confessions of Valmont's had such a ring of truth that Madame de Franval could not help being convinced. Valmont was an excellent match for her daughter; after Eugénie's bad conduct, was it not even more than she had a right to expect? Valmont had undertaken to do everything, and there was no other way of putting an end to the horrible crime that was driving her to despair. Furthermore, could she not hope for a return of her husband's affection after the termination of the only affair that had ever become really dangerous for her and for him? These considerations decided her. She accepted Valmont's offer, but on condition that he would give his word not to fight a duel with her husband, to go to a foreign country after having brought Eugénie to Madame de Farneille, and to stay there until Franval had become calm enough to console himself for the loss of his illicit love affair and consent to Eugénie's marriage.

Valmont agreed to everything. Madame de Franval answered for her mother's intentions and assured him that she would not oppose in any way the decisions they had just made. He left, after again apologizing to her for having taken part in her unscrupulous husband's schemes against her.

Madame de Farneille, having been informed of these plans, left for Picardy the next day, and Franval, caught up in the constant whirlwind of his pleasures, firmly relying on Valmont and no longer fearing Clervil, fell into the trap with the same guilelessness he had so often wanted to see in others when he desired to catch them in one of his own traps.

For about six months, Eugénie, who was now nearly seventeen, had been going out rather often alone or with a few of her friends. On the evening before the day when Valmont was to attack Madame de Franval by arrangement with her husband, Eugénie had gone alone to see a new play at the Théâtre Française, and she was still alone afterward, when she was on her way to the house where she was to meet her father, so that they could go together to another house where they were going to have supper. Shortly after her carriage had left the Faubourg Saint-Germain, ten masked men stopped the horses, opened the door, seized her and put her in a post chaise beside Valmont, who took every precaution to prevent her from crying out, ordered the post chaise to set off at the greatest possible speed, and was out of Paris in the twinkling of an eye.

It had unfortunately been impossible to get rid of Eugénie's servants and carriage, so Franval was notified very quickly. To place himself out of danger, Valmont had counted on Franval's uncertainty as to the road he had taken, and on the two or three hours' head start that he would surely have. If he could reach Madame de Farneille's estate, that would be all that was necessary, because two trustworthy women and a stagecoach were waiting there to take Eugénie toward the border to a refuge unknown even to him, while he would go on to Holland and return only to marry her, as soon as her mother and grandmother notified him that there were no longer any obstacles. But fate allowed these wise plans to be disrupted by the horrible designs of the evil man with whom we are dealing.

When he received the report of Eugénie's servants, Franval did not waste a moment. He went to the post house and asked for what roads horses had been given since six o'clock. At seven o'clock, a berlin coach had left for Lyons; at eight, a post chaise for Picardy. Franval did not hesitate: the berlin coach going to Lyons was surely of no interest to him, but a post chaise headed toward a province where Madame de Farneille had some estates was certainly what he was seeking; to doubt it would have been madness.

He quickly had the eight best post horses harnessed to his carriage, had his servants mounted on small saddle horses, bought and loaded pistols while the horses were being harnessed, and set off with the speed of an arrow toward where he was drawn by love, despair and thirst for vengeance. When he changed horses at Senlis he learned that the post chaise he was pursuing had just left. He ordered top speed. Unfortunately for him, he caught up with the post chaise. He and his men, pistol in hand, stopped Valmont's postilion. As soon as he recognized his adversary, the impetuous Franval shot him dead before he could defend himself, put Eugénie, weak from terror, into his carriage, and was back in Paris before ten o'clock in the morning.

Not worried by what had just happened, Franval was concerned only with Eugénie. Had the treacherous Valmont tried to take advantage of the circumstances? Had Eugénie remained faithful? Were her sinful bonds still intact? She reassured him: Valmont had only revealed his plan to her, and, hopeful of marrying her soon, had refrained from profaning the altar on which he wanted to offer pure vows.

Franval was reassured by her oaths. But what about his wife? Did she know about the plot? Had she taken part in it? Eugénie had had time to make inquiries; she told him that everything had been the work of her mother, whom she called the most odious names, and that her fateful meeting with Valmont, during which Franval had thought that he was serving him so well, had actually been the occasion when he was most insolently betraying him.

"Ah, I wish he still had a thousand lives!" said Franval, furious. "I'd snuff them all out, one after another! And my wife! . . . When I was trying to lull her, she was the first to deceive me! That creature whom everyone thinks so gentle, that angel of virtue. . . . Ah, traitress, you'll pay dearly for your crime! My vengeance must have blood, and, if necessary, I'll draw it with my own lips from your faithless veins. . . . Be calm, Eugénie," he went on in a violent state, "you need rest now. Go and sleep a few hours, I'll handle all this alone."

Meanwhile Madame de Farneille, who had posted spies along the road, soon learned what had happened. Knowing that her granddaughter had been recaptured and that Valmont had been killed, she hurried back to Paris. Furious, she immediately assembled her advisors. They pointed out to her that Valmont's murder was going to place Franval in her hands, that the influence she had been fearing was going to vanish in an instant, and that she would then regain control of her daughter and Eugénie. But they urged her to prevent a public scandal, and, for fear of a dishonoring trial, to solicit an order that would put her son-in-law out of the way.

Franval was immediately informed of this advice and of the action that was being taken in consequence. Having learned that his crime was known and that his mother-in-law was waiting to take advantage of his disaster as soon as it befell him, he went to Versailles without delay, saw the Minister and told him everything. The Minister's only reply was to advise him to leave Paris immediately and go into hiding on an estate he owned in Alsace, near the Swiss border.

Franval returned home. In order to make sure that he could carry out his vengeance and punish his wife for her betrayal, and to be in possession of hostages so dear to Madame de Farneille that she would not dare to take action, politically at least, against him, he resolved to take his wife and daughter with him when he left for Valmor, the estate to which the Minister had advised him to go. But would his wife consent to accompany him? Feeling herself guilty of the betrayal that was the cause of everything that had happened, would she be willing to go so far away? Would she dare to entrust herself without fear to her outraged husband? Such were Franval's apprehensions. To learn if they were justified, he went straight to his wife, who already knew everything.

"Madame," he said calmly, "you've plunged me into an abyss of adversity by your thoughtless indiscretions. Although I condemn their effects, I approve of their cause, which surely lies in your love of your daughter and of me; and since the first wrongs were committed by me, I must forget those that followed. Dear and loving light of my life," he went on, kneeling before her, "will you accept a reconciliation that nothing will ever be able to break again? I've come to offer it to you, and here's what I'll give you to seal it." He laid at her feet all the forged letters of her alleged correspondence with Valmont. "Burn all this, my dear, I beg you," he said with feigned tears in his eyes, "and forgive what jealousy made me do. Let's banish all bitterness between us. My guilt is great, I confess it; but who knows whether Valmont, to succeed in his plans, may not have painted you an even blacker picture of me than I deserve? If he dared to say that I'd stopped loving you or that you hadn't always been the most precious and praiseworthy person in the world to me, if he sullied himself with that calumny, my dear angel, then I did well to rid the world of such a vile impostor!"

"Oh, monsieur," said Madame de Franval, in tears, "the atrocities you've devised against me are almost inconceivable! How do you expect me to trust you after such horrors?"

"I want you to go on loving me, most tender and gracious of women! I want you to accuse only my head and my many failings, and believe that my heart, in which you've always reigned, has never been capable of betraying you. Yes, I want you to know that there isn't one of my errors that hasn't brought me closer to you. The more I forsook my dear wife, the more clearly I saw how irreplaceable she was. No pleasures or sentiments equaled those which my inconstancy was making me lose with her, and in the very arms of her image I missed her reality. . . . Ah, dear and divine wife, where else could I find a soul like yours? Where else could I savor the pleasures that I find in your arms? Yes, I abjure all my errors. I want to live only for you, and to restore in your wounded heart the love I so unjustly destroyed by the sins which I now renounce, even in memory."

It was impossible for Madame de Franval to resist such loving words from the man she still adored. Can one hate what one has truly loved? Could any woman with her delicate and sensitive soul have remained unmoved by the sight of the man who had been so precious to her, kneeling at her feet, his eyes filled with tears of remorse? A sob burst from her throat. "I've never stopped idolizing you," she said, pressing hands to her heart, "and yet you've cruelly driven me to despair. Heaven is my witness that of all the afflictions I received from you, the fear of having lost your heart, or of being suspected by you, was the most painful. And with whom have you outraged me? With my daughter! It's by means of her that you pierce my heart. Do you want to force me to hate the girl whom nature has made so dear to me?"

"I want to bring her back to you," Franval said still more ardently. "I want her to kneel before you and abjure her insolence and her sins, as I have done, and I hope you'll forgive us both, so that the three of us can devote our lives to making one another happy. I'm going to give you back your daughter; give me back my wife, and let us flee . . ."

"Flee? Good heavens!"

"My adventure is stirring up a scandal; tomorrow may be too late for me. . . . The Minister and all my friends have advised me to go to Valmor. Will you go there with me, my angel? At the very moment when I'm begging your forgiveness at your feet, will you break my heart with a refusal?"

"You frighten me . . . What! Your unfortunate adventure . . ."

"It's being treated as a murder, not as a duel."

"Dear God, and I'm the cause of it! Give me your orders, my dear husband, I'm at your disposal: I'll go with you to the ends of the earth if necessary . . . Ah, I'm the most unfortunate of women!"

"No, you're the most fortunate, because from now on every moment of my life will be devoted to changing into flowers the thorns I've placed on your path. If two people love each other, they can find happiness in a desert. Besides, our exile won't last forever: my friends have been notified, and they're going to act."

"But my mother . . . I'd like to see her. . . ."

"No, don't do it, my dear! I have undeniable evidence that she's stirring up Valmont's family against me, that she's personally trying to persuade them to have me arrested. . . ."

"She's incapable of it. Stop imagining such perfidious horrors. Her soul, made for loving, has never known deceit. You've never appreciated her, Franval. If only you could have loved her as I do! We could have found happiness on earth in her arms; she was the angel of peace that heaven offered to the errors of your life. Your injustice rejected her heart, always open to your affection, and, whether from thoughtlessness, caprice, ingratitude or libertinism, you voluntarily deprived yourself of the best and most loving friend that nature had created for you. . . . You really don't want me to see her?"

"No, I beg you not to. Time is so precious! You'll write to her, you'll tell her of my repentance, and perhaps she'll yield to my remorse, perhaps some day I'll recover her esteem and her heart. The storm will eventually die down, and we'll come back . . . We'll come back to enjoy her forgiveness and affection in her arms . . . But we must go now, my dear, there's not a moment to lose. The carriages are waiting for us."

Madame de Franval, frightened, did not dare to raise any more objections. She began preparing to leave: a desire on Franval's part was an order to her. He hurried to Eugénie and brought her back. The false-hearted creature threw herself at her mother's feet with as much duplicity as her father. She wept, begged forgiveness, and obtained it. Madame de Franval embraced her; it is difficult for a woman to forget that she is a mother, no matter how greatly she has been sinned against by her children; the voice of nature is so imperious in a sensitive soul that a single tear from one of those sacred eyes is enough to make her forget twenty years of error or wickedness.

They left for Valmor. The extreme haste in which the journey had to be undertaken was sufficient reason to Madame de Franval, still as credulous and blind as ever, for the small number of servants that her husband had taken with him. Crime shuns the eyes of others; it fears them all: since its security is possible only in the shadows of mystery, it wraps itself in them when it wants to act.

Nothing made her change her mind when they arrived at the country estate. Constant attentions, deference, consideration, respect, demonstrations of affection on one side, of the most violent love on the other—all this, lavished on poor Madame de Franval, delighted and deceived her. Far from her mother in a remote region, living in the midst of terrible isolation, she was happy because, she said, she had her husband's heart, and because her daughter, always at her knees, was concerned solely with pleasing her.

Eugénie and her father no longer had adjoining rooms: his was at the far end of the castle, hers was near her mother's; and at Valmor all the disorders of Paris were replaced to an eminent degree by decency, regularity and modesty. Franval went to his wife's room every night, and there, in the bosom of innocence, candor and love, he insolently dared to nourish hope with his horrors. Cruel enough not to be disarmed by the naïve and burning caresses of the most delicate of women, it was from the torch of life itself that the vile rogue lighted that of vengeance.

As will be readily imagined, however, he had not diminished his attentions to Eugénie. Every day, during her mother's morning toilet, she met him in a secluded part of the garden, where he gave her the instructions she needed for her conduct of the moment, and the favors which she was far from willing to yield entirely to her rival.

Less than a week after their arrival at this refuge, Franval learned that Valmont's family was prosecuting him with fierce determination, and that his crime was going to be treated in the most serious manner. It had become impossible, he was told, to pass it off as a duel: there had unfortunately been too many witnesses. Furthermore, added his informant, there could be no doubt that Madame de Farneille was at the head of his enemies and was intent on completing his ruin either by having him imprisoned or by forcing him to leave France, so that she could bring about the immediate return of the two loved ones who were now separated from her.

Franval showed these letters to his wife; she instantly took up her pen to calm her mother, urge her to adopt a different way of thinking, and describe to her the happiness she had been enjoying ever since misfortune had softened her poor husband's heart. She added that any efforts to make her return to Paris with her daughter would be in vain, that she was determined not to leave Valmor until her husband's difficulties had been resolved, and that if the malice of his enemies or the foolishness of his judges should cause a dishonoring judgment to be pronounced against him, she was firmly resolved to expatriate herself with him.

Franval thanked her; but, having no desire to await the fate that was being prepared for him, he told her that he was going to spend some time in Switzerland, that he would leave Eugénie with her, and that he wanted them both to stay at Valmor until his future was decided; no matter what it should prove to be, he said, he would return to spend twenty-four hours with his dear wife and consult with her about going back to Paris if there was nothing to prevent it, or, if things had gone badly, about going to live somewhere in safety.

When he had made these decisions, Franval did not lose sight of the fact that his wife's insolent plot with Valmont was the cause of his setbacks, and he was still consumed with his desire for revenge. He sent word to Eugénie that he would be waiting for her in the garden. He took her into an isolated summer house, made her swear blind obedience to all the orders he was going to give her, kissed her and spoke to her as follows:

"You're going to lose me, my daughter, perhaps forever..." He saw tears in her eyes. "Be calm, my angel: our fate is in your hands, and, if you're willing, we can live together almost as happily as before, in France or elsewhere. You are, I assume, firmly convinced that your mother is the sole cause of our difficulties. As you know, I haven't given up my vengeance; if I've concealed it from her, you've known the reasons, you've approved of them, and you've helped me form the veil that prudence required us to place before her eyes. The time has come to act, Eugénie. Your security depends on it, and what you're going to do will guarantee mine forever. You understand me, I hope, and you're intelligent to be alarmed for even an instant by what I'm proposing to you. Yes, my daughter, the time has come for action without delay and without remorse, and it's you who must carry it out.

"Your mother has tried to make you unhappy; she has defiled the bond she lays claim to, and so she has lost the rights that go with it. She has therefore become not only an ordinary woman to you, but your deadliest enemy. The law of nature that is most deeply engraved in our hearts is that we must rid ourselves, if we can, of those who conspire against us. That sacred law, which constantly moves and inspires us, does not place love of others above the love we owe ourselves. First ourselves, then others: that is the order of nature. Consequently we must show no respect or consideration for others if they have proved that our unhappiness or our ruin is the only object of their desires. To act differently, my daughter, would be to prefer others to ourselves, which would be absurd. And now, let's come to the reasons that determine the action I'm going to advise you to take.

"I must go away, and you know why. If I leave you with that woman, within a month her mother will have succeeded in persuading her to bring you back to Paris, and since it's no longer possible for you to be married after the scandal that has taken place, you can be sure that those two cruel women will use their power over you to make you spend the rest of your life in a convent, weeping over your weakness and the loss of our pleasures. It's your grandmother who's prosecuting me, Eugénie, it's she who has joined my enemies to help them crush me. Can her conduct have any other goal than to regain possession of you? And if she succeeds, won't she be sure to have you placed in confinement? The worse my case becomes, the more those who are tormenting us will increase their strength and influence. Now you may be sure that your mother is inwardly with them and will rejoin them as soon as I'm gone. However, that group wants to ruin me only in order to make you the unhappiest of women; we must therefore hasten to weaken it, and it will be deprived of its greatest energy if your mother is removed from it.

"Could we adopt another course of action? Could I take you with me? Your mother, enraged, would rejoin hers, and from then on, Eugénie, we'd never have a moment's peace. We'd be sought and pursued everywhere, no country would have a right to give us sanctuary, no refuge on earth would be sacred and inviolable in the eyes of those monsters whose anger would pursue us. Do you know how far those odious weapons of despotism and tyranny can reach when they're directed by malice and supported by gold?

"On the other hand, if your mother is dead, Madame de Farneille, who loves her more than she does you, and who has acted only for her sake in everything, will have lost the only person who attached her to her faction; she'll therefore abandon everything and stop goading my enemies and rousing them against me. Then one of two things will happen: either the Valmont case will be settled and there will no longer be anything to prevent us from returning to Paris, or else it will become worse, and although we'll have to leave France, at least we'll be safe from Madame de Farneille's persecution. As long as your mother is alive, your grandmother's only goal will be to ruin our lives, because, as I've already said, she thinks her daughter's happiness can be built only on our downfall.

"No matter how you look at our position, you'll see that your mother stands in the way of our security, and that her detestable existence is an insurmountable obstacle to our happiness.

"Eugénie," continued Franval, taking her hands, "dear Eugénie, you love me; will you let fear of an act that's so essential to our interests deprive you forever of the man who adores you? Dear and loving Eugénie, you must decide: you can keep only one of us. You must kill one of your parents; you can only choose which heart your criminal dagger will pierce. Either your mother will die or you'll have to give me up . . . What am I saying? You'll have to kill me with your own hand. Alas, could I live without you? Do you think it would be possible for me to exist without my Eugénie? Could I withstand the memory of the pleasures I've savored in your arms, knowing that they were lost to me forever? Your crime will be the same in either case: you must destroy a mother who abhors you and lives only for your unhappiness, or else you must kill a father who breathes only for you. Choose, Eugénie, and if it's I whom you condemn, don't hesitate, ungrateful daughter: pierce without pity this heart whose only sin is too much love; I'll bless the blows that come from your hand, and I'll adore you with my last breath."

Franval waited for her reply, but she seemed lost in deep reflection. Finally she threw herself into his arms and cried, "Ah, you whom I'll love all my life, can you doubt my choice? Can you suspect my courage? Arm me now, and the woman who's condemned by her horrible deeds and her threat to your safety will soon fall beneath my blows! Instruct, direct my conduct, then leave, since your security requires it. I'll act during your absence, and I'll inform you of everything. But no matter what turn things may take, don't leave me alone in this castle once our enemy has been disposed of, I insist on it. Come back here and take me away, or let me know where I can join you."

"My precious daughter," said Franval, kissing the monster he had seduced too well, "I was sure you'd find within you the sentiments of love and firmness necessary to our mutual happiness. . . . Take this box, death is inside it . . ."

Eugénie took the sinister box and renewed her promises to her father. Other arrangements were made: it was agreed that she would await the outcome of the trial, and that whether or not the crime took place would depend on what was decided for or against her father. They parted. Franval went to his wife and carried audacity and deceit to the point of weeping during his farewells to that heavenly angel, and receiving her touching and candid caresses without giving himself away. Then, when she had assured him that she would remain in Alsace with Eugénie, no matter what turn his case might take, the scoundrel mounted his horse and rode away from the innocence and virtue he had sullied so long by his crimes.

Franval went to stay in Basel, where, safe from any legal action that might be taken against him, he was also as close to Valmor as possible, so that his letters would be able to maintain the frame of mind in which he wanted to keep Eugénie while he was away. It was over sixty miles from Basel to Valmor, but communication was so easy, even though the road went through the Black Forest, that he would be able to receive news from her once a week. To deal with any eventualities, he had brought an enormous sum of money with him, but more in paper than in cash. Let us leave him in Switzerland and return to his wife.

Nothing could have been purer or more sincere than that good woman's intentions; she had promised her husband to stay at Valmor until further orders from him, and nothing could have made her decide to do otherwise, as she assured Eugénie every day. Unfortunately too far away from giving her worthy mother the confidence she ought to have felt for her, and still sharing the injustice of her father, who nourished its seeds with regular letters, Eugénie did not think she could have a greater enemy in the world than her mother. And yet there was nothing the latter did not do to destroy the aversion to her which her ungrateful daughter still had in her heart; she lavished caresses and friendship on her, she tenderly expressed satisfaction to her over her husband's fortunate change of heart, sometimes being so sweet and gracious as to thank Eugénie and give her all the credit for that happy conversion; and then she would grieve over having been the innocent cause of the new disasters that were threatening Franval. Far from accusing Eugénie, she blamed only herself, and, clasping her to her bosom, asked her with tears in her eyes whether she could ever forgive her.

Eugénie's appalling soul resisted this angelic behavior; that perverse soul no longer heard the voice of nature: vice had closed every avenue by which it could be reached. She would coldly withdraw from her mother's arms, look at her with wild eyes and say inwardly, to encourage herself, "How hypocritical that woman is!

How treacherous she is! She caressed me in the same way on the day when she had me abducted. . . ." But these unjust reproaches were only the abominable sophisms with which crime supports itself when it wants to stifle the voice of duty. In having Eugénie abducted for the sake of her happiness, for her own peace of mind, and in the interest of virtue, Madame de Franval had, it is true, concealed her plans, but such feints are condemned only by the culprit who is deceived by them; they do not offend honesty. Eugénie resisted all of Madame de Franval's affection because she wanted to commit an atrocity, and not at all because of any wrongs on the part of her mother, who surely had none with regard to her.

Toward the end of the first month of their stay at Valmor, Madame de Farneille wrote to her daughter that her husband's case was becoming extremely serious, and that, in view of the possibility of an adverse judgment, it was quite urgent that she and Eugénie should return to Paris, not only to impress the public, who were saying very bad things, but also to join with her in soliciting a settlement that would disarm justice, and answer for the culprit without sacrificing him.

Madame de Franval, who had decided to hide nothing from Eugénie, showed her this letter immediately. Eugénie stared at her and calmly asked her what she intended to do in view of that sad news.

"I don't know," replied Madame de Franval. "But what good are we doing here? Wouldn't we be much more useful to your father if we followed my mother's advice?"

"That's for you to decide, madame," said Eugénie. "My role is to obey you, and you can count on my submission."

Seeing from the curtness of Eugénie's reply that this idea did not suit her, Madame de Franval told her that she was going to continue writing, that she would write again, and that she could be sure that if she acted contrary to Franval's intentions it would be only with the extreme certainty of being more useful to him in Paris than at Valmor.

Another month went by. Franval continued writing to his wife and daughter and receiving letters from them that were most pleasing to him, because in his wife's he saw only perfect acquiescence to his desires, and in his daughter's he saw wholehearted determination to carry out the projected crime as soon as a turn of events required it, or as soon as Madame de Franval seemed to be yielding to her mother's urging. "If I see only honesty and frankness in your wife," Eugénie wrote in one of her letters, "and if the friends working on your case in Paris succeed in settling it, I will turn over to you the task you have assigned to me and you will perform it yourself if you then see fit. If, however, you find it indispensable for me to act and you order me to do so, I will take care of everything, you may be sure of it."

In his reply, Franval approved of everything she had said, and these were the last letters that each wrote to the other. The next mail brought nothing. Franval became worried. When the following mail also failed to bring him a letter, he sank into despair, and since his natural agitation would not permit him to wait any longer, he immediately decided to go to Valmor in person to learn the cause of the silence that was disquieting him so cruelly.

He set off on horseback, accompanied by a faithful servant. He intended to arrive on the second day, late enough at night not to be recognized by anyone. At the edge of the woods which surrounded his castle at Valmor, and which joined the Black Forest toward the east, six well-armed men stopped him and his servant and asked for his purse. These bandits had been alerted in advance: they knew to whom they were speaking, and they knew that Franval, involved in a dangerous affair, never went anywhere without his portfolio and an enormous amount of gold. The servant resisted and was stretched out lifeless at the feet of his horse. Franval leapt to the ground, sword in hand, and attacked the robbers. He wounded three of them and found himself surrounded by the others; they took everything he had, though without succeeding in disarming him, and hurried away as soon as they had despoiled him. He followed them for a time, but they fled swiftly with their booty and the horses, and it soon became impossible to tell in what direction they had gone.

It was a terrible night. There was a cold north wind, it was hailing, and all the elements seemed to be loosing their fury against the wretched Franval. There are perhaps cases in which nature, revolted by the crimes of the man she is pursuing, wishes to overwhelm him with all the scourges at her command, before drawing him back into her bosom.

Half naked, still holding his sword, Franval left that baleful place as best he could and walked in the direction of Valmor. Being unfamiliar with the environs of the estate, which he had visited only the one time when we have seen him there, he wandered along the dark roads of that forest which was totally unknown to him. Exhausted, racked by pain, consumed with anxiety and tormented by the storm, he threw himself on the ground, and there the first tears he had ever shed in his life welled up abundantly in his eyes.

"Luckless man that I am," he cried out, "everything has combined to crush me at last, to make me feel remorse! . . . It was only through disaster that it was able to penetrate my soul. Deceived by the sweetness of good fortune, I would always have scorned it. O you whom I have offended so grievously, you who are perhaps at this very moment becoming the victim of my fury and my barbarity, adorable wife, does the world, proud of your existence, still possess you? Has the hand of heaven put a stop to my horrors? . . . Eugénie, my too credulous daughter, too shamefully seduced by my abominable wiles, has nature softened your heart? Has she suspended the cruel effects of my domination and your weakness? Is there still time? Is there still time, merciful heaven?"

Suddenly the doleful and majestic sounds of bells, sadly rising into the clouds, came to increase the horror of his fate. He was deeply moved, and frightened . . .

"What do I hear?" he cried, standing up. "Is it death, barbarous daughter, is it vengeance? Is it the Furies of hell coming to finish their work? Do those sounds announce . . . Where am I? Can I hear them? O heaven, finish destroying the sinner!" He prostrated himself. "Dear God, allow me to join my voice to those that are now imploring you. . . . See my remorse and your power, forgive me for having shunned you, and deign to grant my prayer, the first prayer I have ever dared to make to you! Supreme Being, preserve virtue, protect the woman who is your most beautiful image in this world! May those sounds—so mournful, alas!—not be those which I dread!"

And Franval, distraught, no longer knowing what he was doing or where he was going, uttering only incoherent words, walked blindly along the first road he encountered. He heard something; he recovered his senses and listened. It was a man on horseback.

"Whoever you are," said Franval, walking toward him, "whoever you may be, take pity on a poor wretch distracted by grief. I'm ready to take my own life . . . Tell me where I am, help me, if you're a man, and compassionate . . . Please save me from myself!"

"Dear God!" replied a voice that was all too familiar to Franval. "What! You here? Good heavens! Go away!"

And Clervil—for it was that respectable clergyman, escaped from Franval's dungeon and sent by fate at the saddest moment of his life—leapt off his horse and threw himself into the arms of his enemy.

"It's you, monsieur," said Franval, embracing that honorable man, "it's you, against whom I've committed so many atrocious acts for which I must reproach myself!"

"Calm yourself, monsieur; I disregard the sorrows that have just surrounded me, I no longer remember those you inflicted on me, now that heaven has allowed me to be useful to you. . . . And I'm going to be useful to you, monsieur, in a way that's cruel, no doubt, but also necessary. . . . Let us sit down . . . Let us place ourselves at the foot of that cypress: its sinister leaves are the only wreath that now befits you. . . . Oh, my dear Franval, I have so much bad news to tell you! Weep, my friend, your tears will relieve you; and I must bring others to your eyes that will be still more bitter. . . . Your days of pleasure are over; they've vanished like a dream, and you now have only days of grief."

"Oh, monsieur, I understand! Those bells . . ."

"They're carrying to the Supreme Being the homage and prayers of the sad inhabitants of Valmor, whom the Almighty allowed to know an angel only so that they could pity her and mourn her loss. . . ."

Franval put the point of his sword to his heart and was about to end his own life when Clervil forestalled that desperate act.

"No, no, my friend," he said, "it's not death that's called for, but reparation! Listen to me; I have many things to tell you, and you need to be calm to hear them."

"Very well, monsieur, speak, I'm listening: thrust the dagger into my heart by degrees; it's only fair that I should feel some of the pain I was so eager to inflict on others."

"I'll be brief with regard to myself," said Clervil. "After several months of the cruel imprisonment you imposed on me, I was fortunate enough to arouse the pity of my guard, and he released me. I strongly urged him to conceal the injustice you'd committed against me. He won't reveal it, my dear Franval, he'll never say a word about it."

"Oh, monsieur . . ."

"Listen to me; I repeat that I have many things to tell you. When I returned to Paris I learned of your unfortunate adventure and of your departure. I shared Madame de Farneille's tears; they were more sincere than you believed. I joined that worthy lady in trying to persuade Madame de Franval to bring Eugénie back to us, since their presence was more necessary to us in Paris than in Alsace. You'd forbidden her to leave Valmor, and she obeyed you. She told us of your orders and of her reluctance to violate them; she hesitated as much as she could. . . . Then you were convicted, Franval, and your conviction still stands. You've been condemned to death as guilty of a murder on the highway. Neither Madame de Farneille's solicitations nor the efforts of your friends and relatives were able to turn aside the sword of justice: the fatal judgment was against you. . . . You're forever dishonored, you're ruined, all your property has been seized . . ."

Franval again made a desperate movement.

"Listen to me, monsieur," said Clervil, "I demand it of you as a reparation of your crimes, I demand it in the name of heaven, which your repentance may still move to pity. . . . We then wrote to Madame de Franval and told her everything. Her mother announced that since her presence had become indispensable, she was sending me to Valmor to convince her that she had to leave. I followed the letter, and it was unfortunate that it arrived before me, because it was already too late when I came. Your horrible plot had succeeded all too well. I found Madame de Franval dying . . . Oh, monsieur, what an atrocity! But I won't reproach you any more for your crimes, because I'm touched by your state. . . . I'll tell you everything. Eugénie was unable to withstand that sight; when I arrived, she was already expressing her repentance with bitter sobs and tears . . . Oh, monsieur, how can I describe the cruel effect of that scene? Your wife was dying, disfigured by the convulsions of pain . . . Eugénie, returned to nature, was uttering terrible cries, confessing her guilt, invoking death, wanting to give it to herself, falling at the feet of those she was imploring, pressing herself to her mother's bosom, trying to revive her with her breath, to warm her with her tears, to touch her heart with her remorse . . . Such was the sinister scene that struck my eyes when I entered your house.

"Madame de Franval recognized me. She clasped my hands, wetted them with her tears and spoke a few words that were difficult for me to hear, for they could scarcely escape from that chest constricted by the palpitations of the poison. She excused you, she prayed for you, above all she begged forgiveness for her daughter. Yes, cruel man, the last thoughts and wishes of the woman whose heart you lacerated were for your happiness. I cared for her to the best of my ability and urged the servants to do the same. I sent for the most celebrated doctors. I lavished my consolations on your Eugénie; touched by her terrible state, I felt I had no right to refuse them to her. But nothing succeeded. Your poor wife died amid shudders and torments impossible to portray.

"At that fatal moment, monsieur, I saw one of the sudden effects of remorse that had been unknown to me till then. Eugénie threw herself on her mother and died at the same time. At first we thought she had merely fainted; but no, all her faculties were extinguished. The shock had annihilated all her organs at once; she had actually died from the violent impact of remorse, grief and despair. . . .

"Yes, monsieur, they're both lost to you. Those bells whose sounds still strike your ears, are tolling for the two women, both born for your happiness, whom your heinous crimes made victims of their attachment to you, and whose agonizing image will pursue you to your grave. Oh, my dear Franval, was I wrong to try to persuade you to rise from the depths into which your passions had plunged you? Will you still condemn and ridicule the votaries of virtue? Are they wrong to worship it when they see crime surrounded by so much turmoil and disaster?"

Clervil stopped speaking. He looked at Franval and

saw that he was petrified with grief. His eyes were staring fixedly; tears were flowing from them, but no expression was able to reach his lips. Clervil asked him the reason for his half-naked state. Franval gave him a brief explanation.

"Ah, monsieur," cried the magnanimous Clervil, "I'm so glad that I can at least relieve your condition, even in the midst of the horrors that surround me! I was going to see you in Basel, tell you everything and offer you the little I possess. . . . Accept it, I beg you; I'm not rich, as you know, but here's two thousand francs. It's all my savings, it's all I have. I insist that you . . ."

"Generous man!" cried Franval, embracing the knees of that rare and virtuous friend. "Do I need anything after the losses I've just suffered? And yet it's you, whom I've treated so badly, it's you who've come to my aid!"

"We mustn't remember past wrongs when the man who did them to us is overwhelmed by misfortune; the only vengeance we ought to take on him is to help him. And why should we add to his suffering when his heart is torn by his reproaches? That's the voice of nature, monsieur; you can see that the holy worship of a Supreme Being isn't opposed to it as you thought, since the counsels of the former are the sacred laws of the latter."

"No, monsieur," said Franval, standing up, "I no longer need anything. In leaving me this last possession," he went on, holding up his sword, "heaven has indicated the use I'm to make of it." He looked at it. "Yes, my dear and only friend, this is the same sword that my angelic wife seized and tried to thrust into her heart one day when I was crushing her with horrors and calumny. . . . It's the same one. . . . I might even find traces of that holy blood on it. . . . My own blood must efface them. . . . Let us continue along this road until we come to a cottage in which I can communicate my last wishes to you, and then let us part forever."

They began walking, seeking a road that would lead them to a house. The forest was still wrapped in the shades of night. Suddenly the two men heard a mournful chant and saw torches piercing the darkness, giving it a tinge of horror that can be imagined only by sensitive souls. The tolling of the bells grew louder, mingling with the woeful voices that were still scarcely audible. Then lightning, which had not appeared till now, flashed in the sky, and thunder joined the ominous sounds that could already be heard. The lightning that rent the clouds, occasionally eclipsing the sinister flames of the torches, seemed to be contending with the inhabitants of the earth for the right to take to her grave the woman who was being accompanied by that procession. Everything gave rise to horror, everything breathed desolation; nature herself seemed stricken with eternal grief.

"What's that?" said Franval, deeply moved.

"Nothing," replied Clervil, taking his friend's hand and trying to lead him in another direction.

"No, you're deceiving me, I want to see what it is. . . ."

Franval ran forward. He saw a coffin.

"Merciful heaven!" he cried. "There she is, it's she, it's she! God has allowed me to see her again!"

Clervil saw that it was impossible to calm the wretched Franval. In response to his entreaties, the priest walked away in silence.

Franval, distraught, ran to the coffin and took out the sad remains of the woman he had so sorely offended.

He picked up her body, placed it at the foot of a tree and threw himself on it in a frenzy of despair.

"O you whose life has been destroyed by my cruelty," he cried deliriously, "winsome woman whom I still idolize, see your husband at your feet, daring to ask for mercy and forgiveness. Don't think it's because I want to live on after you; no, it's so that the Almighty, touched by your virtues, may forgive me as you have done, if that is possible. . . . You must have blood, my dear wife, it will take blood to avenge you. And you will be avenged. . . . But see my tears first, and see my repentance. I'm going to follow you, beloved spirit. . . . But who will receive my tortured soul if you don't beg mercy for it? Do you want it to be cast from the arms of God and from your bosom, and condemned to the most excruciating torments of hell, when it repents so sincerely of its crimes? Forgive them, dear soul, and see how I avenge them!"

With these words, Franval, having escaped from Clervil's gaze, thrust his sword through his body twice. His impure blood flowed onto his victim and seemed to sully her much more than it avenged her.

"O my friend," he said to Clervil, "I'm dying, but I'm dying in the bosom of remorse. Tell those I leave behind of my deplorable end and of my crimes; tell them that thus must die a poor slave of his passions who has been vile enough to stifle the voice of duty and nature. Don't refuse to let me share my poor wife's coffin; I wouldn't have deserved it without my remorse, but it has made me worthy of that favor, and I demand it. Farewell."

Clervil granted Franval's wish and the procession continued on its way. An eternal refuge soon received a husband and a wife who were born to love each other and know happiness, and would have savored it in its purest form if the sinful hand of one of them had not brought crime and its frightful disorders to change all the roses of their life into serpents.

The honorable clergyman soon returned to Paris with the story of that multiple catastrophe. No one was distressed by Franval's death: it was only his life that caused sorrow. But his wife was bitterly mourned; and indeed, what person is more precious, more appealing in the eyes of men, than one who has cherished, respected and cultivated virtues in this world, only to find misfortune and grief at every step of life's way?

Miss Henrietta Stralson

or

The Effects of Despair
An English Story

One evening when London's Ranelagh was in all its splendor, Lord Granwell, about thirty-six years old, the wickedest, cruelest and most dissolute man in England, and unfortunately one of the richest, was sitting at a table with three of his friends, dulling his remorse with punch and champagne. He noticed a lovely young woman passing by, whom he had never seen before.

"Who is that girl?" he eagerly asked one of his companions. "And how can such a pretty little face have been in London without my seeing it till now? I'll wager she's no more than fifteen. What do you say, Sir James?"

Sir James: "She has a figure like one of the Graces! Don't you know her, Wilson?"

Wilson: "This is the second time I've seen her. She's the daughter of a Hereford baronet."

Granwell: "I don't care if she's the devil's daughter! I must have her, or may lightning strike me dead! Gave, I want you to act as my scout."

Gave: "Miss Henrietta Stralson. That tall woman you see with her is her mother. Her father is dead. For a long time now she's been in love with a Hereford gentleman named Williams. They're going to be married. Williams has come here to collect an inheritance from an old aunt. It constitutes his entire fortune. Lady

Stralson decided to show her daughter London during Williams' stay here. When his affairs are settled, the three of them will go back to Hereford, where the wedding is to take place."

Granwell: "May all the Furies of hell take my soul if Williams touches her before I do! I've never seen anything so pretty . . . Is Williams there too? I don't know the scoundrel, point him out to me."

Wilson: "There he is, behind them. He probably stopped to talk with some of his acquaintances. He's catching up with them . . . Look at him . . . There, that's Williams."

Granwell: "That tall, handsome young man?"

Wilson: "Precisely."

Granwell: "My God! He must be only twenty!"

Gave: "He's truly a handsome man, my lord. There's a rival . . ."

Granwell:: "Whom I shall get rid of, as I have done with so many others. . . . Gave, stand up and follow that angel. Really, she's made an impression on me . . . Follow her, Gave, try to learn everything you can about her, put spies on her trail. Have you any money? Here's a hundred guineas. By tomorrow I expect you to have spent it all and told me everything. . . . Could it be that I'm in love? What do you think, Wilson? One thing is certain: as soon as I saw that girl I had a presentiment . . . Sir James, that heavenly creature will have either my fortune or my life."

Sir James: "Your fortune, perhaps, but as for your life . . . I don't think you have any inclination to die for a woman."

Granwell: "No . . ." He shuddered involuntarily,

then went on: "It's only a figure of speech, my friend. One doesn't die for those animals. But it's still true that there are some of them who can stir up a man's soul in an extraordinary way! . . . Waiters! Bring some Burgundy. . . . My head is aflame and I can cool it only with that wine."

Wilson: "Can it be, my lord, that you're about to let yourself be carried away to the point of destroying poor Williams' happiness?"

Granwell: "What do I care about Williams? What do I care about the whole world? Let me tell you something, my friend: when a fiery heart conceives a passion, there's no obstacle that can prevent it from satisfying itself. The more obstacles I encounter, the more ardent I become. Possessing a woman is flattering to me only in proportion to the number of restraints I've broken to obtain her. There's nothing more commonplace than possessing a woman, my friend. When you've had one you've had a hundred. The only way to break the monotony of those insipid triumphs is to owe them only to ruse, and we can find charm in them only on the wreckage of a multitude of conquered prejudices."

Wilson: "Wouldn't it be better to try to please a woman, to obtain her favors from the hands of love, rather than possessing her by violence?"

Granwell: "What you say would be good if women were more sincere. But since there's not one of them in the world who's not false and treacherous, we must treat them like the vipers that are used in medicine: we must cut off their heads to have their bodies; we must take, at any cost, the little good that can be derived from their physical being, and constrain their moral being in such a way that we can never feel its effects."

Sir James: "Those are maxims that I like."

Granwell: "Sir James is my pupil, and some day I shall make him a subject . . . But here's Gave coming back; let's hear what he has to say."

After drinking a glass of wine, Gave sat down and said to Granwell, "Your goddess is gone. She got into a hired carriage with Williams and Lady Stralson, and they told the driver to go to Cecil Street."

Granwell: "What! So close to my house? . . . Did you have them followed?"

Gave: "I put three men on their trail, three of the wiliest rogues who ever escaped from Newgate.*"

Granwell: "Well, Gave, is she pretty?"

Gave: "She's the most beautiful girl in London. Stanley, Stafford, Tilner, Burkley—they've all followed her, they've all hovered around her, and they all agree that there's not another girl in the three kingdoms who can compare to her."

Granwell (*eagerly*): "Did you hear her say anything? Did she speak? Did the sweet sound of her voice fall on your ears? Did you breathe the air she'd just purified? Speak! Speak, my friend! Can't you see that my head is spinning, that I must have her or leave England forever?"

Gave: "I heard her, my lord. She spoke, she told Williams that it was hot at the Ranelagh and that she would rather go home than continue walking here."

Granwell: "And Williams?"

Gave: "He seems to be strongly attached to her. He devoured her with his eyes. . . . It was as though love had chained him to her side."

---

* A London prison.

Granwell: "I detest that rascal, and I'm afraid circumstances may force me to do away with him. . . . Let's go, my friends. Wilson, I thank you for your information. Keep this a secret, or I'll spread the story of your affair with Lady Mortmart all over London. And you, Sir James, meet me tomorrow in the park and we shall go to see that little opera dancer. . . . What am I saying? No, I won't go. I have only one idea in my head. . . . Nothing in the world but Miss Stralson can interest me, I have eyes only for her, I have a soul only to adore her . . . You, Gave, come and dine with me tomorrow and tell me everything you've been able to learn about that heavenly girl, the sole arbiter of my fate . . . Good-by, my friends."

Granwell got into his carriage and hurried off to the king's bedchamber to fulfill the duties of his position.

Nothing could have been more accurate than the few details Wilson had given about the beauty who had turned Granwell's head.

Miss Henrietta Stralson, born in Hereford, had indeed come to see London, with which she had not been acquainted, while Williams was settling his affairs, and afterward they were going to return home, where their vows were to be sanctified by marriage.

And it is not surprising that Miss Stralson had won such favor with everyone present at the Ranelagh; when a girl has an enchanting figure, soft, bewitching eyes, the most beautiful hair in the world, lively and delicate features, a delightful voice, and a great deal of wit, graciousness and vivacity, tempered by an air of modesty and virtue which makes these charms still more exciting, and when she has all this at the age of seventeen, she is sure to please. Henrietta had therefore created a prodigious sensation, and everyone in London was talking about her.

As for Williams, he was what is called an honest young man—good, upright, without cunning or duplicity. He had worshiped Henrietta since childhood and all his happiness depended on possessing her some day. To support his claim to do so, he had sincere feelings, a considerable fortune if he won his lawsuit, a lineage somewhat inferior to hers but honorable nonetheless, and a very attractive face.

Lady Stralson was also an excellent person. She considered her daughter the most precious thing she had in the world and loved her like a true provincial mother, for all sentiments become perverted in capital cities; virtue deteriorates as one breathes their pestilential air, and since the corruption is general, one must either flee or become infected.

Granwell, overheated by wine and love, was no sooner in the king's antechamber than he realized that he was in no condition to present himself. He went home and, instead of sleeping, began making wild and absurd plans for possessing the object of his passionate rapture. After considering and rejecting a hundred of them, each more atrocious than the one before, he finally decided on this one: he would attempt to turn Williams and Henrietta against each other and, if possible, to create so many difficulties for Williams that it would take him a long time to extricate himself from them; in the meantime, he would seize every opportunity of being with Henrietta, either to dishonor her in London or to abduct her and take her to one of his estates near the Scottish border, where he would have her completely in his power and nothing could prevent him from doing

as he wished with her. This plan suited the treacherous
Granwell best because it involved an adequate number
of atrocities; and so the next day he made all his arrangements for carrying it out.

Gave was Lord Granwell's intimate friend. Endowed with even baser feelings than Granwell's, he
served him in that capacity, so common today, which
consists in furthering the passions of others, multiplying
their debaucheries, and profiting from their follies while
losing one's own honor. He did not fail to meet Granwell
the next day, but the only information he could offer at
that time was that Lady Stralson and her daughter were
staying on Cecil Street, as had already been discovered,
with one of their relatives, and that Williams was staying
in the Poland Hotel in Covent Garden.

"Gave," said Lord Granwell, "I'm counting on you
to deal with Williams. Tomorrow I want you to arrive
at that foul rascal's hotel dressed like a Scotsman and
using a Scottish name. Strike up an acquaintance with
him, then rob him, ruin him. . . . Meanwhile I shall be
at work with the ladies, and you'll see, my friend, that
in less than a month we shall disrupt all the honorable
little plans of those virtuous country folk."

Gave was careful not to find anything wrong with
his protector's plans; the venture would require large
sums of money, and it was clear that the more Granwell
spent, the more lucrative it would be for the infamous
minister of his whims. And so he prepared to act, while
Granwell, for his part, carefully surrounded Henrietta
with a multitude of subordinate agents who were to give
him precise reports on everything she did.

Miss Stralson was staying with Lady Wateley, a
relative of her mother's who had been a widow for the
past ten years.

Enchanted by Henrietta, whom she had not known until her stay in London, Lady Wateley neglected no opportunity of showing off the object of her affection and pride. But this gracious cousin, kept in her room by an inflammation of the lungs, had not only been unable to take part in the last visit to the Ranelagh but was even going to be deprived of the pleasure of accompanying Lady Stralson and her daughter to the opera, where they were to go the following day.

As soon as Granwell's spies had informed him of this forthcoming visit to the opera, he decided to take advantage of it. From a more detailed report he learned that Henrietta and her mother were going to use a hired carriage, since Lady Wateley needed her horses in case she should have to send for her doctor. He went to the owner of the carriage and easily arranged for one of its wheels to break when it was three or four streets from where the ladies would depart. He did not stop to consider that such an accident might take the life of the girl he cherished; concerned only with his stratagem, he paid liberally to have it carried out and joyfully returned home. He left just when he had been told that Henrietta was about to leave. He ordered his coachman to go and wait in the vicinity of Cecil Street until he saw a carriage of a certain description leave Lady Wateley's house, to begin following it as soon as he saw it, and not to let himself be cut off from it by any other carriage.

Granwell was sure that when the ladies left their cousin's house they would stop by for Williams at the Poland Hotel. They did indeed set out in that direction, but they did not go far without incident. The wheel broke, the ladies screamed, one of the footmen broke a limb. Granwell, to whom nothing mattered as long as he succeeded, immediately stopped beside the disabled carriage, leapt out of his own, presented his hand to Lady Stralson and offered her the use of his carriage.

"You're very kind, my lord," she replied. "These hired carriages are frightful in London; one travels in them at the risk of one's life. Steps ought to be taken to remedy the situation."

Granwell: "Allow me not to complain of it, madam, since you and the young lady with you have apparently escaped injury, and I have gained the precious privilege of being of service to you."

Lady Stralson: "You're most obliging, my lord. . . . But my footman seems to be badly injured. This accident has greatly upset me."

Granwell immediately had some chairmen summoned and ordered them to take the injured servant in their sedan chair. The ladies sent him home, then got into Granwell's carriage with him and headed for the Poland Hotel.

It would be difficult to depict Lord Granwell's feelings when he found himself beside the girl he loved, under circumstances which made him appear to be rendering her a service.

"Are you going to the Poland Hotel to visit some foreign lady?" he said to Henrietta when the carriage set off.

"It's much more than that, my lord," Lady Stralson said candidly. "We're going to see my daughter's beloved, her future husband. . . ."

* * *

Granwell: "How distressed your daughter would have been if that accident had delayed the pleasure she's been looking forward to! And how much more grateful I am for the good fortune of being able to serve her!"

Miss Stralson: "You're very kind to concern yourself with us, my lord. We deeply regret having inconvenienced you, and I'm sure my mother will allow me to tell you that I'm afraid we've committed an indiscretion."

Granwell: "It's unjust of you to take such a view of the greatest pleasure of my life. But if I myself may commit an indiscretion, let me ask you whether you won't need my carriage in order to continue your activities this afternoon. If so, shall I be fortunate enough to have you accept it?"

Miss Stralson: "That would be too presumptuous of us, my lord. We were going to the opera, but we shall spend the evening with the friend we're on our way to see."

Granwell: "You can best repay me for my service, which you yourselves have acknowledged, by allowing me to continue it. I beg you not to deprive yourselves of the pleasure on which you had been counting. Melico* will sing today for the last time; it would be a pity to miss this chance of hearing him. And you won't be inconveniencing me in any way, because I, too, am going to the opera; you'll merely be permitting me to accompany you there."

It would have been impolite of Lady Stralson to refuse Granwell, so she did not, and they arrived at the Poland Hotel. Williams was waiting for the ladies. Although Gave had arrived at the hotel that day, he was

---

* A famous Italian *castrato*.

not to begin playing his part until the following day; our young man was therefore alone when the ladies came. He received them as well as he could and overwhelmed Lord Granwell with courtesies and expressions of gratitude; but since time was pressing, they soon went to the opera. Williams gave Lady Stralson his arm. Because of this arrangement, which Granwell had anticipated, he was able to talk with Henrietta. He found that she had infinite wit, extensive knowledge, refined taste—everything that he might have had difficulty in finding in a girl of the highest rank who had never left London.

After the opera, Granwell took the two ladies back to Cecil Street. Lady Stralson, having had reasons only to think highly of him, invited him into her cousin's house. Although Lady Wateley knew him only very slightly, she gave him a warm welcome. She asked him to stay for supper, but he was too adroit to thrust himself forward in that way, so he claimed to have some important business to attend to and left, a thousand times more passionately aflame than ever.

A character like Granwell's does not usually like to languish. Difficulties stimulate it, but those which cannot be overcome extinguish the passions in such a soul instead of making them burn more hotly. And since this kind of man needs constant sustenance, the object would no doubt change if the idea of triumph were to be hopelessly destroyed.

Granwell saw clearly that since it might take him a long time to turn Williams and Henrietta against each other, while he was working toward that goal he should also be trying to set the charming girl at odds with her mother, for he was certain that he could never carry out his plan as long as they were united. Once he had been introduced into Lady Wateley's house, it seemed

impossible to him, especially since he would still have
the help of his agents, that any of Henrietta's actions
should escape him. He therefore devoted all his attention
to his new plan of disunion.

Three days after the opera incident, Granwell went
to inquire about the ladies' health. He was surprised
to see Lady Stralson come into the parlor alone. She
conveyed Lady Wateley's apologies to him for being
unable to invite him to come upstairs, due to ill health.
Annoyed though he was, Granwell showed great interest in Lady Wateley's condition. But he could not refrain
from asking about Henrietta. Lady Stralson replied that,
having been somewhat shaken by the carriage accident,
she had been staying in her room. A short time later
Granwell asked permission to return; he then left, highly
dissatisfied with his day.

Meanwhile Gave had become acquainted with
Williams, and on the day after Granwell's fruitless
visit to Lady Wateley's house he came to report on
his activities.

"I've furthered your plans more than you think,
my lord," he said. "I've seen Williams and some law-
yers who know all about his case. The inheritance he's
expecting, the inheritance that composes the fortune he
hopes to offer to Henrietta, is quite capable of being
contested. In Hereford there's a closer relative who isn't
aware of his rights. We must write to that man to come
at once, guide him when he's here, and place him in possession of the inheritance. In the meantime I'll empty the
purse of that insolent individual who dares to set himself
up as your rival. He's opened himself to me with a candor that befits his age: he's already told me about his
love; he's even talked to me about you and the kindness
you showed his sweetheart the other day. He's caught,

I assure you. You can place the matter entirely in my hands and I guarantee you that the fool will be ours."

"That news consoles me a little for what happened to me," said Granwell, and he told his friend about the way he had been received at Lady Wateley's. "Gave," he continued, "I'm madly in love; all this is taking a long time and it's impossible for me to restrain my violent desire to possess that girl. . . . Listen to my new plan; listen to it, my friend, and carry it out at once: tell Williams that you'd like to know the girl he adores, and that since you can't go to see her in the house of a woman you don't know, he must pretend to be ill and urge her to come to him in a sedan chair. Work on that, Gave, work on it without neglecting the rest, and let me act in accordance with your progress."

Gave, the cleverest knave in England, was completely successful in his undertaking. Without losing sight of the over-all plan, and while seeing to it that a letter was written to Squire Clark, the second heir of Williams' aunt, telling him to come to London immediately, he persuaded his friend to let him see Henrietta, and in precisely the way proposed by Granwell. Miss Stralson was informed that Williams was ill; she sent word to him that, on the pretext of making some purchases, she would find time to go to see him. Lord Granwell was instantly notified from two directions that on Tuesday at four o'clock in the afternoon Miss Stralson would go to Covent Garden alone in a sedan chair.

"Ah, you whom I idolize, this time you won't escape me!" exclaimed Granwell, overjoyed. "Consoled by the pleasure you will give me, I shall feel no remorse over the means I shall use to possess you, no matter how violent they may be. Remorse? Can such feelings ever enter a heart like mine? The practice of evil has long since extinguished them in my hardened soul. You multitude of other beauties seduced like Henrietta, deceived like her, abandoned like her—tell her whether I was moved by your tears, whether your struggles frightened me, whether your shame softened me, whether your charms held me! Yes, she's going to be one more name on the list of the illustrious victims of my debauchery. And what else are women good for? I defy anyone to prove that nature created them for anything else. Let fools have their ridiculous mania for raising them to the rank of goddesses. It's with such meek principles that we make them insolent; seeing us place so much value on their trifling favors, they feel that they have a right to value them highly also, and so they make us waste time in romantic lamentations when we ought to be devoting ourselves entirely to pleasure ... Ah, what am I saying, Henrietta? One look from your eyes of flame will destroy my philosophy, and perhaps I shall fall at your feet even while I am swearing to defile you ... What! Can *I* know love? Away, vulgar sentiment! If there were one woman in the world who could make me feel it, I think I'd shoot her rather than submit to her infernal wiles. No, no, weak, deceitful sex, don't ever hope to capture me; I've enjoyed your pleasures too often to be still impressed by them. It's by provoking the god that one learns to smash the temple, and when one wants to eradicate the cult one can't commit too many outrages."

After these reflections, worthy of a scoundrel like himself, Granwell immediately sent men out to hire all the sedan chairs in the vicinity of Cecil Street. He placed his servants at all the street corners to prevent any sedan chairs that might come in search of a mas-

ter from approaching Lady Wateley's house, then he
sent one of his own chairs, carried by two porters he
could trust, with orders to take Henrietta, once they
had her, to the house of a certain Mrs. Schmidt, near
Saint James's Park. This woman had been devoted to
Granwell's secret adventures for twenty years, and he
had, of course, given her advance notification of his
plans. Without worrying or having any doubts about
what she thought were the public porters she was hiring,
Henrietta, wrapped in a cloak, got into the sedan chair
that was offered to her and asked to be taken to the
Poland Hotel. Not knowing the streets, she was not
troubled by any suspicion during the trip. She arrived
where Granwell was awaiting her. The porters, carefully instructed, turned into the lane leading to Mrs.
Schmidt's house and did not stop until they were before
the door of a low room. The door opened . . .

Imagine Henrietta's surprise when she found herself in a strange house! She cried out and stepped back,
then she told the porters that they had not taken her
where she had ordered.

"Miss Stralson," said Granwell, quickly coming
forward, "how thankful I am to heaven for having
once again placed me in a position to be useful to
you! From what you've said, and from the appearance
of your porters, it's clear that they're drunk and have
made a mistake. Isn't it fortunate that this slight accident
should have happened to you at the house of my cousin,
Lady Edwards? Be so kind as to come in, Miss Stralson,
dismiss those rascals with whom your life isn't safe, and
allow my cousin's servants to find some reliable men
for you."

It would have been difficult to refuse such an offer.
Henrietta had seen Lord Granwell only once, he had

given her no reason to complain of him, and she had now met him again at the entrance to a house which looked quite respectable; even assuming that there was some danger in accepting what had been offered to her, would it not have been still more dangerous to remain in the hands of two drunken men who, irritated by her reproaches, were contemplating abandoning her? She therefore went inside, apologizing profusely to Granwell. He dismissed the porters himself and pretended to order the servants to go and bring others. Miss Stralson was led through several rooms by the mistress of the house. When she had reached an attractive drawing room, the so-called Lady Edwards bowed and said to Granwell with an impudent expression, "Enjoy yourself, my lord! I couldn't have given you a prettier one myself!"

Henrietta shuddered and felt as though her strength were about to fail her. She realized all the horror of her situation, but she was able to control herself: her safety depended on it. She summoned up her courage.

"What do you mean by that, madame?" she said, seizing Mrs. Schmidt by the arm. "And for whom am I being taken here?"

"For a charming girl, Miss Stralson," said Granwell, "for an angelic creature who will soon, I hope, make the most fortunate of men into the most amorous of lovers."

"My lord," said Henrietta, without letting go of Mrs. Schmidt, "I see that my imprudence has placed me in your power, but I appeal to your sense of justice. If you take advantage of my situation, if you force me to hate you, you will surely not gain as much as you would gain from the feelings you have already aroused in me."

"You're a clever girl, but you won't lead me astray with either your enchanting face or the incredible guile that now inspires you. You don't love me, you couldn't love me. I don't lay claim to your love. I know the man who inflames your heart, and I consider myself more fortunate than he. He has only a frivolous sentiment which I shall never obtain from you, whereas I have your delightful body which is about to plunge my senses into ecstasy."

"Stop, my lord, you've been misinformed: I'm not Williams' sweetheart. I've been betrothed to him without the consent of my heart. My heart is free; it can love you as well as anyone else, and it will surely hate you if you try to gain by force what you can earn by merit if you so choose."

"You don't love Williams? Then why were you going to see him? Do you think I don't know that you were on your way to see him because you thought he was ill?"

"That's true, but I wouldn't have gone if my mother hadn't told me to. You can find out for yourself. I was only obeying her . . ."

"Artful creature! . . ."

"Oh, my lord, give in to the feeling I think I see in your eyes now! Be generous; don't make me hate you when you can so easily win my esteem."

"Your esteem?"

"Good heavens, would you prefer hatred?"

"Only a more ardent feeling would soften me."

"Are you so ignorant of a woman's heart that you don't know what gratitude can lead to? Let me go, my lord, and some day you will know whether Henrietta is ungrateful, whether she's worthy of having obtained your pity!"

"What! You expect *me* to feel pity, pity for a woman?" said Granwell, pulling her away from Mrs. Schmidt. "Do you expect me to miss the finest opportunity of my life and deprive myself of the greatest of pleasures in order to spare you a moment of pain? Why should I do such a thing? Come here, siren, I won't listen to you any longer. . . ."

As he said these words he snatched off the kerchief that covered Henrietta's lovely bosom and flung it to the other side of the room.

"Merciful heaven," she cried, throwing herself at his feet, "don't let me become the victim of a man who wants to force me to hate him! . . . Have pity on me, my lord, I beg you to have pity on me! May you be moved by my tears, may your heart still listen to virtue! Don't crush a poor girl who's guilty of no offense against you, in whom you've aroused gratitude, and who might not have stopped at that point . . ."

As she spoke thus she was kneeling at his feet with her arms raised to heaven; tears streamed down her beautiful cheeks, animated by fear and despair, and fell onto her uncovered bosom, a thousand times whiter than alabaster.

"Where am I?" said Granwell, bewildered. "What indescribable emotion is troubling all the faculties of my being? Where did you get those eyes which disarm me? Who lent you that seductive voice, each sound of which softens my heart? Are you a heavenly angel, or are you only human? Speak, who are you? I no longer recognize myself; I no longer know what I want or what I'm doing. My faculties, completely absorbed in you, will let me do nothing except make your wishes my own. . . . Stand up, Miss Stralson, it's I who must fall at the feet of the goddess who has enchained me. Stand up; your dominion is too well established: it's becoming impossible, absolutely impossible, for any impure desire to overthrow it in my heart. . . ." He gave her back her kerchief. "Here, hide that intoxicating beauty from me; I have no need to increase the rapture into which all your charms have plunged me."

"Sublime man!" cried Henrietta, pressing one of his hands. "What do you not deserve for such a generous act?"

"What I want to deserve is your heart, Miss Stralson: that's the only reward I aspire to, the only triumph worthy of me. Remember forever that I had complete power over your body and did not abuse it. . . . And if that doesn't obtain for me the feelings I demand of you, remember that I shall be entitled to take vengeance, and that vengeance is a terrible emotion in a soul like mine. Sit down, Miss Stralson, and listen to me . . . You've given me hope, you've told me that you don't love Williams, you've led me to believe that you could love me—those are the reasons that have stopped me; it's to them that you owe your victory. I prefer to win from you what I could take without your consent. Don't make me regret my virtue, don't make me say that the treachery of men is due only to the duplicity of women, and that if they always behaved toward us as they ought to, we would always treat them as they desire."

"My lord," replied Henrietta, "you cannot fail to recognize the fact that in this unfortunate incident it was you who did the first wrong. By what right have you tried to destroy my peace of mind? Why have you had me brought to a strange house when I had entrusted myself to public servants, assuming that they would take me where I ordered? In view of that, my lord, is it for you to make demands? Should you not apologize to me, instead of imposing conditions on me?" Seeing Granwell make a gesture of dissatisfaction, she added with animation, "Nevertheless, my lord, let me explain myself: your generous, noble sacrifice has made amends for that first wrong, which, if you like, is excused by the love you claim to feel. I undoubtedly owe you gratitude; I have promised to be grateful and I shall keep my word. Come to my family's house; I shall urge them to treat you as you deserve. As I continue to see you, the flame of gratitude that you have lighted in my heart will be constantly rekindled. Your greatest hopes will be justified. . . . You would despise me if I said any more than that. . . ."

"But how will you explain this incident?"

"As it ought to be explained: as a porter's mistake which, by an extraordinary stroke of chance, placed me for the second time in the hands of a man who, having already rendered me one service, was glad to have an opportunity of rendering me another."

"And do you swear that you don't love Williams?"

"It would be impossible for me to hate a man who has never treated me with anything but kindness; he loves me, I can have no doubt of that, but the choice was made by my mother and there's nothing to prevent me from revoking it."

She stood up, then said, "Let me beg you, my lord, to have some porters brought for me. If I stay here any longer it may cast suspicion on me and lessen the plausibility of what I'm going to say. Send me away, my lord, and don't delay in coming to see me. I've been filled with gratitude by your benevolence, and I forgive your barbarous scheme because of the wise and virtuous way in which you've tried to make me forget it."

"Cruel girl!" said Lord Granwell, also standing up.

"Yes, I will obey you. . . . But I'm counting on your heart, Henrietta, I'm counting on it. . . . Remember that when my passions are thwarted they drive me to desperation. To use your own words, don't force me to hate you. There would have been little danger if I'd made you hate me, but the danger will be enormous if you make me hate you."

"No, my lord, I will never force you to hate me. I have more pride than you think, and I shall always be able to keep a right to your esteem."

Granwell summoned the porters who had been waiting nearby. When they were announced, he took Henrietta's hand, led her toward the door and said: "Angelic girl, don't forget that you've just won a victory that no other woman could have dared to hope for, a triumph which you owe only to the feelings you arouse in me, and that if you ever betray those feelings they will be replaced by all the crimes that vengeance can dictate to me."

"Good-by, my lord," Henrietta said as she got into the sedan chair. "Never regret your noble act, and rest assured that heaven and all just souls will owe you a reward for it."

Granwell went home in a state of indescribable inner tumult, and Henrietta returned to her mother in such great agitation that she seemed on the verge of fainting.

If one reflects on Miss Stralson's conduct, one will easily discern that everything she said to Granwell was prompted only by guile and expediency. She felt that it was permissible for her to employ such ruses, ill suited to her ingenuous soul, in order to escape from the dangers that were threatening her. We are confident that no one will blame that winsome girl for having acted as she did; the purest virtue sometimes forces one into certain lapses.

When she reached home, where she no longer had any reason for dissimulation, she told her mother and Lady Wateley everything that had just happened to her; she did not conceal what she had said in order to escape, or the commitments she had been obliged to make for the same purpose. Except for the imprudence of having gone out alone, nothing she had done was disapproved. But her mother and Lady Wateley were opposed to her keeping the promises she had made. It was decided that she would carefully avoid Lord Granwell everywhere, and that Lady Wateley's door would remain firmly closed to the insolent man's attempts to gain admittance. Henrietta felt compelled to say that such conduct would infuriate him, that his desperation might be dangerous, that although he had done wrong he had made amends for it like a gentleman, and that she therefore thought it would be better to receive him than to anger him. She believed she could state that this would also be Williams' opinion. But the two older women would not change their minds, and orders were given accordingly.

Meanwhile, Williams, who had been waiting for Henrietta all evening and was now impatient at not having seen her arrive, left Captain O'Donnel (this was the name that Gave had given himself on coming to the Poland Hotel). He asked him to excuse him so that he could go and determine for himself the cause of Henrietta's absence, which worried him so painfully. He arrived at Lady Wateley's house an hour after Henrietta's return. She wept when she saw him; taking his hand, she said to him tenderly, "Oh, my dear, how close I came to being no longer worthy of you!" And since she was free to talk alone with him as much as she liked, for her mother already considered him as her son-in-law, they were left to discuss together everything that had happened.

"Oh, Henrietta," cried Williams when he had heard her story, "and it was for me that you were about to be ruined! To give me a moment of satisfaction, you were about to make yourself the unhappiest creature on earth! Yes, for a mere whim on my part, for I must confess that I wasn't ill: a friend wanted to see you, and I wanted to enjoy in his presence the good fortune of possessing the affection of such a beautiful woman. That's the whole story, Henrietta. You can see that I'm doubly guilty."

"Let's drop that, my dear," replied Miss Stralson. "I'm with you again, and everything else is forgotten. But you must admit," she went on, letting her eyes ignite a sweet flame in the soul of the man she adored, "that I should never have seen you again if that disaster had befallen me. You would no longer have wanted the victim of such a man, and along with my grief I should have had the despair of losing what is dearest to me in all the world."

"You mustn't think that, Henrietta!" said Williams. "There's nothing under the sun that could prevent you from being dear to the man who places all his glory in possessing you! I will adore you till my last breath! Be assured that the feelings you give rise to are above all human occurrences, and that it's as impossible not to have them as it is that you could ever make yourself unworthy of inspiring them."

The two lovers then discussed the catastrophe more calmly. They realized that Lord Granwell was a very dangerous enemy, and that the course of action which had been decided upon would only serve to embitter him; but there was no possibility of changing it, for the ladies refused to reconsider it. Williams spoke of his new friend, and the two young people were so naïve and trusting that they never even suspected that the false Scotsman might be an agent of Granwell. Far from it: Williams' praises of him made her want to know him, and she was pleased with him for having made such a good acquaintance. But let us leave that worthy couple, who had supper together, consoled each other, made arrangements for the future, and finally parted; let us leave them for a moment and return to their persecutor.

"By hell and all the demons that live in it, I don't deserve to be alive, my friend!" Granwell said to Gave when the latter came to see him the next day. "I'm nothing but a schoolboy, a pitiful fool . . . I held her in my arms, I saw her at my feet, and I never had the courage to make her submit to my desire. . . . It was beyond my power to dare to humiliate her. . . . She's not a woman, my friend, she's a part of the Divinity itself, come down to earth to awaken in my soul virtuous sentiments which I'd never known before in my life. She led me to believe that she might perhaps love me some day, and I, who could never understand how a woman's love could be of any value in the enjoyment of her body, I gave up that enjoyment for the sake of an imaginary sentiment which perturbs and torments me, even though I can't yet understand it."

Gave vigorously reproached Lord Granwell; he made him fear that he had allowed himself to be a young girl's plaything, he assured him that he might not have another such opportunity for a long time, because she would now be on her guard. . . .

"Yes, my lord," he added, "remember that you'll regret the mistake you've just made, and that your indulgence will cost you dearly. Should a man like you be softened by a few tears and a pair of pretty eyes? And will the languid weakness that you've let your soul sink into give you the same amount of sensual pleasure as the stoic indifference you once swore always to maintain? You'll regret your pity, my lord, I promise you . . . By my soul, you'll regret it!"

"We shall soon know," said Lord Granwell. "I shall go to Lady Wateley's house tomorrow without fail. I shall study that clever young lady, I shall examine her, Gave, I shall read her feelings in her eyes, and if she's trying to deceive me, let her beware! I shall not lack tricks to make her fall into my trap again, and she won't always have the magic art of escaping as she did yesterday. . . . As for you, Gave, continue with your plans to ruin that scoundrel Williams. When Squire Clark appears, send him to Sir James; I shall tell Sir James everything, he'll advise Clark to take action to obtain the inheritance that Williams is trying to take away from him, and we shall further his case with the judges. Later, we shall either break off these arrangements, if it becomes certain that my angel loves me, or press them vigorously, if the infernal creature has deceived me. . . . But, I repeat, I've behaved like a child, and I shall never forgive myself for the stupid mistake I've made. Hide that mistake from my friends, Gave, conceal it carefully; they would overwhelm me with reproaches, and all of them would be deserved."

They parted, and the next day, that is, two days after the scene in Mrs. Schmidt's house, Granwell presented himself at Lady Wateley's door in luxury and splendor.

The ladies had not changed their decision. Lord Granwell was harshly refused admittance. When he insisted and sent word that he had to speak to Lady Stralson and her daughter about a matter of the utmost importance, he was told that the ladies he had asked to see were no longer staying in that house. He went away furious. His first impulse was to go to Williams, point out the service he had rendered Henrietta (telling the story as she had agreed on it with him at Mrs. Schmidt's house), and demand that his rival either take him to Lady Stralson or fight a duel with him if he did not share his views. But this plan did not seem cruel enough to him. It was only on Henrietta that he wanted to take vengeance. She had probably not reported things to her family as she had promised; it was only because of her that he had been refused admittance to Lady Wateley's house, she was the only one he wanted to seek out and punish, and that was the only goal toward which he ought to be working.

Although precautions had been taken in Lady Wateley's house, the ladies had no intention of secluding themselves. Lady Stralson and her daughter therefore continued to go out whenever their affairs in London required it, and sometimes, also, merely for their pleasure or the satisfaction of their curiosity. Lady Wateley, now in better health, accompanied them to the theater, where they met a number of their friends. Williams also went there. Granwell, still as well served as ever, was aware of all these movements and tried to make use of them by finding in them some means of satisfying his sinful desires as well as his thirst for vengeance. A month went by without his having found an opportunity, however, although he never ceased working in secret.

Clark had arrived from Hereford and, instructed

by Sir James, had already begun making efforts to get the inheritance, with the powerful support of Granwell and his friends. Poor Williams was harassed by all this, and at the same time the self-styled Captain O'Donnel was swindling and robbing him every day, until he no longer knew which way to turn. But these maneuvers were too slow to suit Lord Granwell's fiery desires. He was still as eager as ever to have a chance to humiliate poor Henrietta. He wanted to see her at his feet again, he wanted to punish her for the stratagem she had employed against him. Such were the baleful schemes brewing in his accursed head when he was informed that Lady Wateley and her guests, who had not been going out in society very much since Williams' affairs had taken such a bad turn, were going the next day to the Drury Lane Theater, where Garrick, who was at that time preparing to retire, was to give his last performance in *Hamlet.*

Granwell's malevolent mind conceived the blackest plan that could have been inspired by his villainy: he resolved to do nothing less than to have Miss Stralson arrested at the theater and taken to Bridewell[*] that same evening.

Let us cast some light on that abominable scheme.

A girl named Nancy, a very famous courtesan, had just escaped from Dublin. After committing a multitude of thefts and publicly leading several Irishmen into disorder, she had fled to England, where, in the short time since her arrival, she had already been guilty of several underhanded crimes, and the officers of the law, armed with a warrant for her arrest, were trying to capture her. Granwell was aware of this. He went to the constable charged with the task of apprehending Nancy and, seeing

---

[*]A prison for immoral women.

that he had only an imperfect knowledge of the girl he had been ordered to arrest, easily persuaded him that she would be at Drury Lane that evening, in the box where Henrietta was going to be sitting. Thus, having been imprisoned in place of the courtesan who was being sought, Henrietta would be at the mercy of his odious designs. He would immediately stand surety for her: if the unfortunate girl consented to his desires, she would be free; if not, he would help Nancy escape from London undetected, strengthen the belief that Henrietta was the adventuress from Dublin, and thus prolong his unhappy victim's captivity indefinitely. He was somewhat troubled by the company in which Henrietta would be found. But Lady Wateley had never seen Lady Stralson and her daughter before their arrival in London, and although she was sure she had relatives by that name in Hereford, it was possible that she had been deceived about their identity. It would be easy to convince her, thought Granwell, that she had made a great mistake. And what argument would she be able to bring forward to defend those women and have them released from prison? When Granwell had worked out this plan in his mind and described it to Gave and Sir James, who examined it from all angles and finally decided that it had no drawbacks, they set about putting it into action. Granwell hurried to the magistrate having jurisdiction over Nancy's case and told him that he had seen her the day before and that she was going to be at Drury Lane that very evening with some honest women whom she had beguiled, and to whom she had dared to present herself as a young lady of quality. The magistrate did not hesitate: orders were given and all arrangements were made to arrest the unfortunate Henrietta in the theater.

Granwell's vile cohorts did not fail to go to the theater that evening; but, as much out of decency as expediency, the members of that infamous troop were to be only spectators. The box became filled: Henrietta sat down between Lady Wateley and her mother; behind them were Williams and Lord Barwill, a friend of Lady Wateley's who was a Member of Parliament and enjoyed great esteem in London. When the play was over, Lady Wateley decided to wait for the rest of the audience to go out before leaving her box; it was as though she had a presentiment of the misfortune threatening her friends. Meanwhile the constable and his men had not lost sight of Henrietta, and Granwell and his associates kept their eyes on the constable. When the crowd had dispersed, Williams gave his arm to Lady Wateley as they left the box, Lady Stralson walked alone, and Barwill was Henrietta's escort. At the end of the corridor, the constable came up to the unfortunate Henrietta with his hand raised, touched her with his rod and ordered her to come with him. She fainted; Lady Wateley and Lady Stralson fell into each other's arms, and Barwill, seconded by Williams, pushed back the officers of the law.

"You're mistaken, you rogues!" cried Barwill. "Step aside or I will have you punished!"

This scene alarmed those who were still inside the theater; they watched and began gathering round. The constable showed his warrant to Barwill, thereby revealing that he believed Henrietta to be Nancy. Then Sir James, prompted by Granwell, came up to Barwill.

"My lord," said that deceitful knave, "allow me to tell you that you will regret having defended this girl of whom you know nothing. I assure you that she is really Nancy from Dublin; I will swear to it if necessary."

Barwill, who had known Lady Stralson and her daughter only a short time, went over to Lady Wateley while Williams was aiding Henrietta.

"Madam," he said, "here is the warrant. This gentleman, in whose integrity I have complete confidence, has assured me that the warrant is justified and that the constable is not mistaken. Please be so kind as to explain all this."

"By everything I hold most sacred, my lord," cried Lady Stralson, "this poor girl is my daughter, she's not the creature who's being sought! Please don't abandon us, please serve as our defender! Devote yourself to the truth, my lord, protect us, come to the aid of innocence!"

"You may withdraw," Barwill said to the constable, "I will answer for this young lady. I myself will take her to the judge without delay. Go and wait for us at his house. You will carry out any new orders he may give you; until then, I will stand surety for Miss Stralson, and your mission is accomplished."

As soon as Barwill had said this, everyone left. The constable went off in one direction, Sir James, Granwell and his troop went off in another, and Barwill led the ladies away, saying, "Let us leave quickly, and not make a spectacle of ourselves any longer."

He gave his arm to Henrietta and the others followed. He and the three women got into his carriage, and a few minutes later they were in the presence of the famous Fielding, the judge in charge of the case.

Considering the testimony of Barwill, who had been his friend for a long time, and listening to the honest and candid replies of the three women, the magistrate could not help seeing that he had been deceived. To convince himself of it still more strongly, he compared

Henrietta's appearance with the written description of Nancy, and when he saw that there were obvious differences he apologized to the ladies courteously and profusely. After expressing their gratitude to Lord Barwill, they left him and peacefully returned to Lady Wateley's house, where Williams was waiting for them.

As soon as she saw him, Henrietta said to him, still filled with emotion, "Ah, my dear, what powerful enemies we have in this cursed city! I wish we had never come to it!"

"There's no doubt," said Lady Stralson, "that it was all the work of that treacherous Granwell. I didn't want to say anything about my ideas before, out of circumspection, but each new reflection supports them: it's impossible to doubt that that blackguard is harassing us this way because he wants revenge. And who knows? It may also be he who has given Williams this new competitor for his aunt's legacy. We scarcely knew Squire Clark in Hereford, no one ever even suspected that relationship, and yet now he's triumphing, he has patronage all over London, and my unfortunate friend Williams may be on the brink of ruin. But no matter," concluded that kind and upright lady, "even if he becomes poorer than Job he will still have my daughter's hand. . . . I promise her to you, my friend, I promise her to you. You alone please the dear child, Williams, and her happiness is all I seek."

Henrietta and Williams, in tears, threw themselves into Lady Stralson's arms and effusively expressed their gratitude to her.

Williams felt guilty, however, and did not dare to admit it. Under the spell of Gave masquerading as Captain O'Donnel, he had lost, either with his false friend or in the circles into which he had led him, nearly all the money he had brought to London. Seeing no connection between Granwell and the Scottish captain, he was far from suspecting that the latter was the former's agent. He said nothing, sighed in silence, received with embarrassment the marks of affection bestowed on him by Henrietta and her mother, and did not dare to confess his failings. He was still hoping that a more fortunate moment might bring back his little fortune. But if that moment never came, and if Clark won the lawsuit, Williams, feeling that he was unworthy of the kindness being lavished on him, was determined to do anything rather than abuse it.

As for Granwell, there is no need to depict his fury: it can easily be imagined.

"She's not a woman," he repeated constantly to his friends, "she's a creature far above humanity.... It will do me no good to plot against her, she will always escape! ... So be it, let her continue; I advise her to do so ... But if my star ever gains ascendancy over hers, she'll pay dearly for the infamous deception she inflicted on me!"

Meanwhile all the plans for poor Williams' ruin had been laid with even more cunning and promptness than usual. The lawsuit over the inheritance was about to be settled, and Granwell spared no effort in the interest of Squire Clark, who, never conferring with anyone but Sir James, did not even suspect who was supporting him so powerfully.

The day after the Drury Lane incident, Granwell went to Fielding to apologize for his mistake. He did so with such good faith that the judge apparently held nothing against him, and the scoundrel went off to invent other ruses which, if successful, would finally ensnare the unfortunate object of his idolatry.

The opportunity was not long in coming: Lady

Wateley had a rather attractive country house between Newmarket and Hosden, about fifteen miles from London; she decided to take Henrietta there to distract her a little from the dark cares that were beginning to trouble her. Granwell, informed of every step taken by Henrietta, learned the date for which her departure had been set. He knew that she and the other two ladies were planning to spend eight days in the country and return on the afternoon of the ninth. He disguised himself, took with him a dozen of those ruffians who walk the streets of London and are willing to become anyone's henchman for a few guineas, and hurried off with these bandits to wait for Lady Wateley's carriage in a corner of a forest not far from Newmarket, famous for the murders that were committed in it every day. The carriage would have to pass by the spot on the way back. It was stopped by force, the traces broke, the servants were beaten, the horses ran away, the women fainted, and Henrietta was carried unconscious into another carriage a short distance away. Her abductor got in with her, the vigorous horses dashed forward, and they were soon in London. Granwell had not revealed his identity to Henrietta or said a word to her on the way. He quickly went into his house with his prey, placed her in a remote room, dismissed his servants and unmasked himself.

"Well, traitress," he said furiously, "do you recognize the man you dared to betray with impunity?"

"Yes, my lord, I recognize you," she replied courageously. "Would it be possible for me not to think of you as soon as a disaster befalls me? You're the sole cause of all those that I've experienced; your only pleasure is to torment me. If I were your deadliest enemy, you would act no differently."

"Cruel woman, isn't it you who have made me the most wretched of men by abusing my good faith? And by your infamous duplicity, haven't you made me the dupe of the feelings I conceived for you?"

"I thought you were more just, my lord: I thought that before condemning people you would at least deign to hear them."

"Do you expect me to let myself be caught a second time by your damnable wiles?"

"Ah, how unlucky I am! I shall be punished for too much frankness and credulity, and the one man in the world whom I have singled out will be the cause of all the catastrophes of my life!"

"What do you mean, Miss Stralson? Explain yourself. I'm willing to listen to your self-justification, but don't hope to deceive me, don't think you can take advantage of that fatal love which ought to fill me with shame. . . . No, Miss Stralson, you won't lead me into error again. . . . You no longer interest me. I see you objectively now, and the only desires you kindle in me are for crime and vengeance."

"Just a moment, my lord: you're accusing me too lightly. A woman who wanted to deceive you would have received you; she would have prolonged your hope, she would have tried to disarm you, and, with the guile you attribute to me, she would have succeeded. . . . Consider how differently I've acted. Discover my reasons and condemn me if you dare!"

"What! During our last meeting you led me to believe that you weren't indifferent to me, you invited me to come to see you—it was on that condition that I restrained myself, and that delicacy replaced in my heart those feelings which you censured—and when I'd done everything to please you, when I'd sacrificed everything to obtain a heart which it would have been useless for me to possess if I'd listened only to my desire, my reward was to have your door closed to me! . . . No, no, treacherous woman, don't hope to escape from me again! Abandon all hope of it, your efforts would be in vain."

"Do whatever you like with me, my lord, I'm at your mercy." (She involuntarily shed a few tears.) "You've no doubt obtained me at the cost of my mother's life. . . . Even so, do as you like with me, I won't use any means of defense. . . . But if you could hear the truth without accusing it of trickery, I would ask you, my lord, if the refusals you received were not certain proof of my feelings for you and the fear to which their power over me gave rise. What need would there have been to keep you away if you had not been feared? And would you have been feared if I had not openly admitted what I felt for you? Take your vengeance, my lord, punish me for having abandoned myself too much to that enchanting error. . . . I deserve all your anger. You can never make its effects too severe, or press them too vigorously."

"Ah!" exclaimed Granwell, in a state of incredible agitation. "I knew this cunning creature would try to capture me again! . . . Oh no, no, you're not in the wrong, Miss Stralson, it's I who am completely to blame! I'm the only one who's guilty, it's my duty to punish myself. I was a monster, because I plotted against a girl who adored me in the depths of her soul. . . . I didn't see it, Miss Stralson, I didn't know. . . . Forgive the extreme humility of my character—how could I have been presumptuous enough to believe that I was loved by a girl like you?"

"This is no time for sarcasm or joking, my lord, so

allow me to tell you that you've made me the unhappiest of women, and I was far from wanting to make you the unhappiest of men. That's all I have to say to you, my lord. It's only natural that you should not believe it. Permit me to have enough pride, humiliated though I am, not to try to convince you of it. It's painful enough for me to have to blush for my failing in front of my family and friends, without having to weep over it with the man who caused it. . . . Don't believe anything of what I've told you, my lord, I've lied to you about everything; I'm the most deceitful woman in the world, you surely can't see me as anything else. . . . No, don't believe me . . ."

"But if your feelings for me were such as you would have me believe, and if it was impossible for you to see me, why couldn't you have written to me? Shouldn't you have assumed that I was greatly upset over the rebuff I'd been given?"

"I'm not independent, my lord; if you bear that in mind you will agree that a girl of my age, whose sentiments have been formed by a good upbringing, must do her best to stifle in her heart everything her family disapproves of."

"And now that you're no longer dependent on that barbarous family, which opposed your wishes as well as mine, will you consent to give me your hand immediately?"

"What! When my mother may be dying as a result of what you've done? No, permit me to think only of her, to whom I owe my life, before concerning myself with my own happiness!"

"Put your mind at rest: your mother is safe. She's in Lady Wateley's house, and they're both as well as you are. My orders to assist them as soon as you'd been taken away were carried out even more capably than those which have placed you in my power. There's no reason for you to have the slightest apprehension on that subject; don't let it interfere in any way with the decisive answer I'm asking you to give me. Will you accept my hand or not?"

"Surely you don't think I would decide such a thing without my mother's approval! I want to be your wife, my lord, not your mistress. Could I rightfully become your wife if, being dependent on my family, I married you without their consent?"

"Let me point out, Miss Stralson, that you're now at my mercy, and that it's not for a slave to try to impose conditions."

"Oh! Then I won't marry you, my lord! I don't want to be the slave of the man my heart has chosen."

"Proud creature, I shall never succeed in humiliating you!"

"Would a triumph over a slave do honor to your sensibility? Can one's self-esteem be flattered by anything brought about by violence alone?"

"It's not always certain that that vaunted sensibility is as precious as women think."

"Leave those harsh principles to men who are unfit to deserve the hearts they try to conquer; such abominable maxims were not made for you."

"But Williams, Miss Stralson, Williams . . . I wish that all the misfortunes with which nature can overwhelm a man were heaped upon the head of that vile rascal!"

"Don't say that about the most honorable of men."

"He deprives me of your heart, he's the cause of everything—I know you love him."

"I've already answered you in that respect, and I

shall continue to tell you the same thing: Williams loves me, and that's all . . . Ah, my lord, if your plans are never opposed by anything more dangerous than that, you won't be as unfortunate as you think you are."

"No, enchantress, no, I don't believe you!" Granwell became overwrought. "Come, Miss Stralson, prepare yourself: I've given you ample time for reflection, and you may be sure that I haven't brought you here to let you make a fool of me again. This very evening you must become either my wife or my mistress."

He seized her roughly by the arm and pulled her toward the profane altar on which he intended to sacrifice her.

"One word, my lord," she said, holding back her tears and resisting his efforts with all her strength, "just one word, I beg you . . . What do you hope to gain from the crime you're about to commit?"

"All the pleasure it can give me."

"You'll have that pleasure for only one day, my lord: tomorrow I shall no longer be either your slave or your mistress, tomorrow you will have before your eyes only the corpse of the girl you've dishonored . . . Oh, Granwell, you don't know my character, you don't know the extremes to which I'm capable of going. If it's true that you have any feeling at all for me, will you buy a quarter-hour of trifling enjoyment at the cost of my death? I offer you the same pleasures you want to take from me by force—why won't you accept them from my heart? You're a just and sensitive man," she went on, half bowing, stretching forth her clasped hands toward her tyrant, "let yourself be moved by my tears! Let my cries of despair reach your soul once again, you won't regret hearing them. Oh, my lord, you see before you, in the attitude of a supplicant, a woman who placed all her glory in the hope of chaining you at her feet some day. You want me to be your wife? Then consider me as such already, and don't dishonor the woman whose destiny is so closely bound up with yours. . . . Return me to my mother, I beg you, and I will repay your kindness with the keenest, most ardent feelings."

Granwell was no longer looking at her; he was pacing back and forth, burning with love, tormented by his thirst for sensual pleasure, gnawed by his craving for vengeance, and assailed by the pity that was born of his love and aroused in his heart, in spite of himself, by Henrietta's sweet voice, appealing posture and abundant tears. Sometimes he was ready to seize her, at other times he was on the point of forgiving her, and it was impossible to tell which of these inclinations was ultimately going to prevail.

Then Henrietta, perceiving his agitation, said to him: "Come, my lord, come and see whether I want to deceive you: take me to my mother yourself, ask her for my hand, and you'll see whether I shall serve your desires."

"Very well, you incomprehensible girl . . . Very well, I will yield to you a second time. But if you're deceiving me again, there's no human force that can protect you from my vengeance. Remember that it will be terrible, that it will cost the blood of those who are dearest to you, and that of all those around you there's not one you won't see lying at your feet, struck down by my hand."

"I accept everything, my lord. Let's go now: don't leave me in my anxiety about my mother any longer. My happiness lacks only her consent, and the knowledge that she's out of danger. Then your desires will be satisfied without delay."

Lord Granwell gave orders to prepare a carriage.

"I shall not go with you," he said to Henrietta. "I'd rather not choose this time to appear before your mother and Lady Wateley; you can see how much I trust you. Tomorrow, at exactly noon, a carriage of mine will come for you and your mother. You'll come to my house, where you'll be received by my family. The notaries will be present and I shall become your husband that same day. But don't forget that if I encounter even the shadow of a refusal, from either you or your relatives, you will have no deadlier enemy in London than I. . . . Go, the carriage is waiting. I shall not even take you to it. . . . I cannot too soon be rid of your gaze, which has such a strange effect on my heart that it urges me to crime and summons me to virtue at the same time."

When she returned home, Henrietta found the whole household in tears. Lady Stralson had been injured on the head and arm, her cousin Lady Wateley was keeping to her bed because of the terrible fright she had received, two servants had nearly been crushed at the scene of the attack. But Granwell had told the truth: as soon as he had left, the same men who had assaulted the carriage had become its protectors. They had caught the horses, helped the women to get back into the carriage, and escorted them to the gates of London.

Lady Stralson wept much more bitterly over the loss of her daughter than over the momentary pain she was experiencing. It was impossible to console her, and serious steps were about to be taken when Henrietta appeared and threw herself into her mother's arms. A few words explained everything, but revealed nothing new to Lady Wateley, who had never doubted that the treacherous Lord Granwell was behind this new disaster. Henrietta related what had happened; her mother and Lady Wateley became still more apprehensive. If they complied with Granwell's invitation, there would be no turning back: Henrietta would have to become his wife the following day. And what an enemy they would have if they refused!

In this terrible perplexity, Lady Stralson wanted to return to Hereford immediately. But would even this have protected that unfortunate mother and her daughter from the wrath of a man who had sworn to pursue them to the ends of the earth if they did not do as Henrietta had promised? Would it have been any safer for them to lodge a complaint and make use of powerful patronage? They could not have done so without doubling the bitterness of a man whose passions were terrible, and whose vengeance was greatly to be feared. Lady Wateley declared herself in favor of the marriage: it would be difficult for Henrietta to find a better match, a lord of the highest rank, and enormously wealthy; and should not the ascendancy she had over him convince her that she would be able to wrap him around her little finger all her life?

But Henrietta's heart was opposed to this solution. All her feelings made Williams still dearer to her and at the same time increased her hatred of the horrible man who was hounding her. She said that she would rather die than accept Lady Wateley's suggestion, and that the terrible necessity of disguising her feelings with Lord Granwell had made him more odious to her than ever. It was therefore decided that she would delay as much as possible, receive Granwell politely, and feed the flames of his passion with hope while at the same time trying to extinguish them with procrastination. In the meantime, when their affairs in London had been settled, she would secretly marry Williams and they would return to Hereford without letting Granwell know of their departure. Once they were there, if that dangerous man continued his persecution of her, the fact that it would now be directed against a married woman would give it a seriousness which would assure Henrietta and her mother of the protection of the law. But would this course of action be successful? Now that the fiery Granwell had already been deceived twice, would he not have good reason to believe that Henrietta was trying to deceive him a third time? And in that case, would she not have to fear the worst from him? These reflections did not occur to her mother and Lady Wateley, however. They held to their plan, and the next day Henrietta wrote to her persecutor that the state of her mother's health would not permit her to carry out the promise she had made; she begged him not to be angry, and to come instead to console her for the regret she felt at not being able to keep her word and for the sadness with which she was filled by her mother's illness.

Granwell's first reaction was one of anger.

"I've been deceived again!" he cried. "Once again I'm the dupe of that false creature. And to think that I had her in my power! I could have forced her to submit to my desires, I could have made her the slave of my will! But I let her triumph. . . . The traitress has escaped from me again. . . . But I shall see what she wants with me. I shall find out whether her mother's condition can serve as a legitimate excuse for her."

When Granwell arrived at Lady Wateley's house, he naturally did not admit that he was the author of the disaster of the day before; he merely said that he had been informed of it and that the interest it was impossible not to have in Lady Stralson as soon as one had the good fortune of knowing her had made him hurry to her to inquire about the state of her health and that of her loved ones. The ladies took their cue from him and continued the conversation in the same tone. A short time later, he took Henrietta aside and asked her if she thought her mother's slight indisposition would cause a long delay in the happiness of their union, and whether he might not venture to make a few proposals to her in spite of it. Henrietta calmed him and begged him not to be impatient. She told him that although her mother and Lady Wateley were hiding their feelings, they were nevertheless convinced that he was the cause of everything they had suffered the day before, and that it was therefore not the right time to open such a discussion.

"Isn't it already a great deal that we've been allowed to see each other?" she said. "And will you again accuse me of deceiving you, now that I've given you permanent admittance to a house you've filled with bitterness and sorrow?"

But Granwell never believed that anyone had done anything for him as long as his desires had not been satisfied. In a voice faltering with emotion, he told Henrietta that he would give her another twenty-four hours, and that he was absolutely determined to know what to expect from her by the end of that time. Then he ended his visit, and this moment of repose will bring us back to Williams, whom we have lost sight of amid the preceding events.

Thanks to the criminal efforts made by Granwell and Gave, poor Williams' lawsuit was going as badly as anyone could imagine. The case was going to be decided in court in a few days, and Squire Clark, apparently supported by every influential person in London, already considered himself, not without reason, as the sole inheritor of the wealth which Williams had expected to bring to the charming Henrietta at the time of their marriage. Granwell neglected nothing which might help to make sure that the case would be decided as he desired. At first, this undertaking had been of only secondary importance, but he now felt that the success of his entire operation depended on it, for he thought it unlikely that Henrietta would consent to marry Williams if he were completely ruined. And even if her sensibility should make her feel obliged to go through with it anyway, her mother would probably not allow her to do so. Despite everything Henrietta had told him during their last conversation, it was impossible for him not to recognize that there had been more cunning and circumspection in her words than tenderness and truth. His spies continued to report to him also, and he could not doubt that the two young people were still seeing each other. He therefore resolved to press Williams' ruin, as much to turn the Stralsons against him as to obtain by this catastrophe a final means of placing Henrietta in his hands, from which he swore that she would never escape again.

As for Captain O'Donnel, after having squeezed everything he could from Williams, he had cruelly abandoned him and withdrawn to Granwell's house, which he left very seldom, for fear of being recognized. His protector had demanded this precaution until the consummation of the entire scheme, which, according to him, would take place within a few days.

Meanwhile, Williams, reduced to his last four guineas, without even enough money to cover the expenses of his lawsuit, had decided to go and confess his faults to the good Lady Stralson and her adorable daughter. He was about to go to them when he was suddenly struck by the final thunderbolt. Judgment was passed on his lawsuit, Clark was recognized as being two degrees more closely related than Williams to the relative whose legacy was being contested, and the unhappy young man found himself with neither the modest fortune he had previously possessed nor the larger one he had hoped to receive. Overwhelmed by his multiple calamities, unable to withstand the horror of his situation, he was ready to take his own life, but it was impossible for him to do so without seeing one last time the only person who had made it dear to him. He hurried to Lady Wateley's house. He knew that Lord Granwell was being received there, and he knew why, but despite his alarm he had not dared to disapprove. In his disastrous position, how could he have imposed his will? In view of the policy now being pursued, it had been agreed that Williams would be received only in secret. He therefore arrived at night, at an hour when he was sure Granwell would not appear. Henrietta did not yet know about the outcome of his lawsuit. He informed her of it, and at the same time he also gave her the distressing news of his gambling losses.

"Oh, my darling Henrietta!" he cried, throwing himself at her feet. "This is my last farewell to you: I've come to release you from your ties, and soon I shall break those which bind me to my life. Treat my rival kindly, don't refuse your hand to him. He alone can make you happy now: my errors and misfortunes have made it impossible for me to belong to you. I urge you as your best friend to become my rival's wife. You must forget a wretched man who is no longer worthy of anything but your pity."

Henrietta drew him to his feet, placed him beside her and said, "Never for one moment have I stopped adoring you! How could you believe that my feelings depended on the whims of fortune? And what an unjust creature I should be if I were to stop loving you because of your imprudent mistakes or your misfortunes! Rest assured that my mother will not abandon you any more than I shall. Let me be the first to tell her everything that's happened to you; I want to spare you the chagrin of confessing it to her. But promise me that you'll live, swear to me that as long as you're sure of my heart, no misfortune can make you end your life."

"Ah, my beloved, I swear it at your feet! What could be more sacred to me than your love? What misfortune can I fear while my Henrietta still cherishes me? Yes, I shall live, since you love me, but don't demand that I marry you, don't bind your fate to that of a wretched man who's no longer worthy of you. Become Lord Granwell's wife. I shall not learn of your marriage without sorrow, but it will at least be without jealousy, and the splendor with which that powerful man will surround you will console me, if that's possible, for not having been able to claim the same happiness."

It was not without tears that the loving Henrietta heard these words; they were so repugnant to her that she could not let Williams continue.

"Unjust man!" she cried, seizing his hand. "Could my happiness exist without yours? And would you be happy if I were in another man's arms? No, no, my darling, I'll never abandon you. I now have one more debt to pay: the one that's imposed on me by your adversity. Before, I was bound to you only by love; I'm now bound to you by duty. I owe you consolation.

From whom would it be dear to you, if not from your Henrietta? Isn't it my hand that ought to wipe away your tears? Why do you want to deprive me of that pleasure? If you had married me with the fortune that was to belong to you, you would have owed me nothing; I'm now attaching you to me with the bonds of love and the tender ties of gratitude."

Williams wetted her hands with his tears, and his excessive emotion prevented him from finding words to express what he felt. Lady Stralson came in while our two lovers, lost in each other's arms, were consumed with a divine flame which passed from one soul to the other. Henrietta told her what Williams did not dare to say, and ended her account by begging her not to change her feelings in any way.

When the good Lady Stralson had learned everything, she threw her arms around Williams' neck and said, "Come, my dear, we loved you rich, and we shall love you even better poor. Never forget your two good friends, and trust them with the task of consoling you. You've made a mistake, my friend. You're young, you have no ties; you'll make no more mistakes when you're the husband of the girl you love."

We shall pass in silence over Williams' expressions of affection. Anyone who has a heart will imagine them without having heard them, and nothing can be conveyed to a cold soul.

"Oh, my dear daughter," said Lady Stralson, "I'm so afraid that in all this there's some new ruse on the part of the horrible man who's been tormenting us. . . . That Scottish captain who ruined our good Williams in such a short time, that Squire Clark whom we'd never known to be related to our dear friend's aunt—these are the schemes of that treacherous man. Ah, how I wish we'd never come to London! We must leave this dangerous city, my daughter, we must go away from it forever."

It is not difficult to believe that Henrietta and Williams adopted this plan with joy. They set a time for their departure: it was decided that they would leave in two days, but that everything would be done in such secrecy that not even Lady Wateley's servants would know about it. When these arrangements had been agreed upon, Williams said that he was going to leave and began making his preparations. Henrietta stopped him.

"Don't forget," she said, handing him a purse filled with gold, "that you've told me the sad state of your finances, and that I alone must place them in order again."

"Oh, Henrietta! Such generosity!"

"She's made me see that I've been remiss," Lady Stralson said to Williams. "Take the purse, my friend, take it. . . . I'll let her enjoy the pleasure of giving it to you today, but on condition that she will never deprive me of it again."

Weeping and filled with gratitude, Williams left, saying to himself, "If happiness can ever be mine on this earth, it will surely be within that honorable family. I've made a mistake, I've suffered a terrible setback. . . . I'm young, the service offers me an expedient. . . . I'll try to make sure my children will never know about this; those precious proofs of the love of the woman I adore will always be the sole concern of my life, and I'll pursue fortune so vigorously that they'll never be affected by my adversity."

Lord Granwell came the next day to visit the girl he loved. She and her mother forced themselves to be polite, as usual, but he was too perceptive not to discern certain differences in their conduct, and too shrewd not to attribute them to the drastic change in Williams' fortune. He made inquiries. Although great secrecy had been maintained about the planned departure and Williams' latest visits, it was impossible that nothing should transpire, and consequently it was not long before Granwell, extremely well served by his spies, was informed of everything.

"Well," he said to Gave when this latest information had been brought to him, "once again I'm the dupe of that band of traitors! While the faithless Henrietta entertains me, she thinks only of gratifying my rival . . . Ah, false and deceitful sex, we're right to outrage you and despise you afterward, and every day your betrayals justify the accusations that are made against you! . . . Gave, my friend, the ingrate doesn't know whom she's offending. I want to take vengeance on her for my whole sex, I want to make her weep tears of blood for her sins and those of all creatures like her. . . . In your dealings with that vile Williams, Gave, have you obtained any samples of his handwriting?"

"Here's one."

"Let me have it . . . Good . . . Take this note to Johnson, that rascal who's so clever at forgery. Tell him to copy in Williams' handwriting the letter I'm going to dictate to you."

Gave wrote out the letter and took it to Johnson, who copied it. At seven o'clock on the evening before her planned departure, Henrietta was given the following letter by a man who told her it was from Williams and that he was impatiently awaiting her reply:

I am about to be arrested for a debt which is much greater than any sum I can obtain. It is

certain that powerful enemies are behind this.
I shall scarcely have time, perhaps, to embrace
you one last time. I am awaiting that happiness,
and your advice. Come alone to the corner of
Kensington Gardens to give a few moments
of consolation to your unhappy Williams, who
is ready to die of grief if you refuse him this
favor.

Henrietta was deeply distressed when she had read this letter. Fearing that such imprudence might finally chill her mother's kindness, she decided to conceal this new catastrophe from her, obtain as much money as she could, and hurry to Williams' aid. For a moment she reflected on the danger of going out at such an hour. . . . But what had she to fear from Lord Granwell? She believed him to be completely taken in by the pretenses of her mother and Lady Wateley. She and the two ladies had not stopped receiving him. He had never seemed calmer. What, then, was there to fear from him? Perhaps he was going to take action against Williams, perhaps he was again the cause of this new calamity; but she told herself that a man's desire to harm a rival he still regarded as a threat was no reason for him to try to destroy the freedom of the woman he ought to trust.

Weak, unhappy Henrietta, such was your reasoning! Love suggested it to you and justified it at the time; you did not realize that the veil before the eyes of lovers is never so thick as when the abyss is about to open beneath their feet. . . .

Henrietta sent for a sedan chair and went to the appointed place. The sedan chair stopped. It was opened . . .

"Miss Stralson," said Granwell, offering her his hand to help her get out, "I'm sure you weren't expecting me here. You will no doubt say that the scourge of your life is constantly appearing before your eyes. . . ."

She screamed and tried to break away and flee.

"Be calm, my pretty angel, be calm," said Granwell, placing the end of a pistol against her chest and showing her that she was surrounded. "Don't hope to escape from me, Miss Stralson. I'm tired of being your dupe, I must have revenge. . . . Be silent, or I won't answer for your life."

Henrietta, unconscious, was carried to a post chaise. Granwell got into it with her and they traveled at top speed, without stopping for a minute, until they reached the isolated castle he owned in the north of England, on the Scottish border.

Gave remained behind in Granwell's town house, with orders to keep watch and send swift couriers with precise news of everything that took place in London.

Lady Stralson did not become aware of her daughter's absence until two hours after her departure. Sure of Henrietta's conduct, she was not worried at first, but when she heard the clock strike ten she shuddered and began to suspect some new trap. She hurried to Williams and asked him, trembling, if he had seen Henrietta. His answer increased her alarm. After telling Williams to wait for her, she went to Lord Granwell's house. She was told that he was ill. She announced who she was, certain that he would receive her when he heard her name. She was given the same reply. Her suspicions redoubled. She returned to Williams and, terribly agitated, they both went immediately to see the Prime Minister, to whom they knew that Granwell was related. They recounted their misfortunes to him and told him that the man who had been so cruelly disrupting their lives, who was the sole cause of everything that had happened to them, and who was the abductor of Lady Stralson's daughter and Williams' fiancée, was none other than Lord Granwell.

"Granwell!" the Prime Minister exclaimed in astonishment. "But do you realize that he's my friend, my relative, and that while I grant you that he may be somewhat irresponsible, I can't believe him to be capable of such abominable conduct?"

"But he's the one who's done it, my lord, it's he!" replied the grief-stricken mother. "Investigate and you'll see whether or not we're deceiving you."

A messenger was immediately sent to Granwell's house. Gave, not daring to lie to an emissary of the Prime Minister, sent word to him that Granwell had gone off to make a tour of his estates. This report, combined with Lady Stralson's suspicions and complaints, finally opened the Prime Minister's eyes.

"Madam," he said to her, "go home with your friend and set your mind at rest; I'm going to act. You may be sure that I shall make every effort to bring back your daughter and restore the honor of your family."

But all these steps had taken time, and the Prime Minister did not wish to take any judicial action before receiving the advice of the King, to whom Granwell was attached by his position. These delays made it possible for Gave to send a courier to his friend's castle; as a result, the events which remain to be described were able to take place without hindrance.

On reaching his estate, Granwell had calmed Henrietta enough to make her agree to take a little rest; but he had been careful to place her in a room from which it was impossible to escape. In her painful state, she had little desire to sleep, but she was glad to have an opportunity of being left in peace for a few hours, so when Gave's courier arrived she had not yet made any kind of sound which might lead anyone to suspect that she was awake. From that moment on, Granwell realized that if he wanted to succeed he would have to act swiftly. He did not care what means he employed; he was resolved to do anything, no matter how criminal it might be, provided it would assure him of obtaining his vengeance and enjoying his victim. At worst, he told himself, he would marry her and not appear in London until after he had become her husband. But from what Gave's courier had just told him, he saw clearly that in his present situation he would not have time for anything unless he quelled the storm that was gathering above his head. He saw that two things were necessary in order to do this: to calm Lady Stralson and to make sure of Williams. An abominable ruse and a heinous crime would accomplish both these things, and Granwell, who shrank from nothing when the satisfaction of his desires was at stake, had no sooner conceived these horrible plans than their execution became his sole concern. After telling the courier to wait, he went to Henrietta. He began by making insulting propositions which she deftly evaded as usual. This was what he wanted: he hoped that she would employ all her wiles, so that he could pretend to succumb to them again, and then catch her in the same traps she had previously used against him. She did everything she could to overthrow the plans he presented to her: tears, entreaties, love, everything was brought forward indiscriminately, and after much opposition Granwell pretended to give in to her and treacherously fell at her feet.

"Cruel girl," he said, wetting her hands with feigned tears of repentance, "your ascendancy over me is too

great, you always triumph. I surrender forever, at last . . .
It's all over now, Miss Stralson: you'll never again see me
as your persecutor, you'll always see me as your friend.
I'm more generous than you think; I want to make the
utmost efforts of courage and virtue with you. You can
see everything I have a right to demand, everything
I could ask in the name of love, everything I could
obtain by violence—well, Henrietta, I renounce it all!
Yes, I want to make you respect me, and miss me,
perhaps, some day . . . I want you to know that I've
never been taken in by you: despite all your pretenses,
I know you love Williams. You're going to receive him
from my hand. At that price, shall I obtain forgiveness
for all the harm and suffering I've inflicted on you? In
giving you Williams, and in using my own fortune to
make up for the setbacks which his has just undergone,
shall I acquire some right to my dear Henrietta's heart,
and will she still call me her cruelest enemy?"

"Oh, generous benefactor!" exclaimed Henrietta,
too quick to seize the illusion that had come to soothe
her for a moment. "What god has inspired you with that
design, and why is it that you've deigned to change my
sad fate so abruptly? You ask what right you will acquire
to my heart? All the feelings of that sensitive heart which
don't belong to poor Williams will be yours forever. I
shall be your friend, your sister, your confidante. Concerned only with pleasing you, I shall dare to ask you
one favor: that of allowing me to spend my life near
you, and to spend each moment of it in showing you
my gratitude. . . . Think carefully, my lord: aren't the
feelings of a free heart preferable to those you wanted
to take by force? You would never have made anything
but a slave of the girl who is now going to become your
most affectionate friend."

"Yes, Miss Stralson, you will be that sincere friend," stammered Granwell. "I have so much to make amends for that even with the sacrifice I'm making to you I don't yet dare to consider myself free of debt. I shall count on time and my own behavior."

"What are you saying, my lord? How little you know my soul! It's opened by repentance as readily as it's angered by offenses, and I can't remember wrongs committed by anyone who has taken even a single step to obtain forgiveness for them."

"Very well, then, let everything be forgotten on both sides, and give me the satisfaction of personally preparing the ties you desire so much."

"Here?" asked Henrietta with a surge of anxiety which she could not restrain. "I thought we were going back to London, my lord."

"No, my dear Miss Stralson, I shall make it a point of honor not to take you back there until you're the wife of the rival to whom I'm yielding you. . . . By showing you in public as his wife, I want to let all England know how much your victory cost me. Don't oppose this plan, for I shall find in it my triumph as well as my peace of mind. I want you to write a letter to your mother telling her not to worry, and another to Williams telling him to come here; we shall celebrate your wedding as soon as he arrives, and return to London the following day."

"But what of my mother?"

"We shall ask her consent; she will certainly not refuse it, and it will be Lady Williams who will come to thank her for it."

"Very well, my lord, I'm at your service. Now that I'm so filled with gratitude and affection, is it for me to control the means by which you deign to work for my happiness? Do as you wish, my lord, I give my approval to everything. Absorbed in the feelings I owe to you, and occupied in experiencing and describing them, I've forgotten all those which might distract me from them."

"But you must write, Miss Stralson."

"To Williams?"

"Yes, and to your mother. Would anything I could say to her persuade her as well as what you'll write to her yourself?"

Writing materials were brought in and she wrote the two following letters:

From Henrietta to Williams:

Let us both fall at the feet of the most generous of men. Come and help me show him the gratitude we owe him. No sacrifice was ever nobler, or more gracious, or more complete: Lord Granwell wishes to unite us himself, it is his hand which will bind us together. Come quickly! Embrace my mother, obtain her consent, and tell her that her daughter will soon enjoy the happiness of clasping her in her arms.

From Henrietta to her mother:

The most dreadful anxiety has given way to the sweetest calm: Williams will show you my letter, most adored of mothers. I beg you not to oppose your daughter's happiness or Lord Granwell's intentions, which are as pure as his heart. Good-by; forgive your daughter if, totally given over to gratitude, she is scarcely able to express her fervent feelings for the best of mothers.

To these letters Granwell joined two of his own: he assured Williams and Lady Stralson of his happiness in uniting two people whose fondest friend he wanted to become, and he told Williams to go to his lawyer in London and collect ten thousand guineas, which he begged him to accept as a wedding present. These letters were full of affection, and they were written in such a frank and guileless tone that it was impossible not to believe them. At the same time, Granwell wrote to Gave and his friends to still the public uproar, calm the Prime Minister and spread word that London would soon see how he made amends for his misdeeds. The courier left with his dispatches. Granwell devoted himself to overwhelming Henrietta with kindness and courtesy, in order, he said, to do his best to make her forget all the crimes against her with which he had to reproach himself. And in the depths of his soul, the monster gloried in having at last been able to use his cunning to triumph over the girl who had so long kept him in bondage with her own.

The courier sent by Henrietta's abductor reached London just after the King had advised the Prime Minister to take strong judicial action against Granwell. But Lady Stralson, thoroughly deceived by the letters she had received, and believing their contents all the more easily because she had become accustomed to Henrietta's victories over Granwell, hurried to the Prime Minister. After telling him everything that had occurred, she begged him not to prosecute Granwell. The proceedings were dropped and Williams prepared to leave.

"Be tactful with that powerful and dangerous man," Lady Stralson said to him, embracing him. "Enjoy the triumph my daughter has won over him, then come back, both of you, and console the mother who adores you."

Williams left, but without taking the lavish gift that Granwell had offered him. He did not even inquire whether that sum was waiting for him or not; such an act would have had the appearance of doubt, and those good and honest people were far from having any.

Williams arrived . . . Dear God! He arrived, and my pen stops, refusing to describe the horrors that awaited the unfortunate lover! Come, Furies of hell, lend me your serpents! Let it be with their flashing tongues that my hand shall set down the horrors which remain for me to tell.

"My dear Henrietta," said Granwell, coming into his captive's room in the morning with an air of happiness and joy, "come and enjoy the surprise I've prepared for you. Hurry, my dear! I want to show Williams to you at the foot of the very altar before which he will receive your hand. Come, he's waiting for you."

"He, my lord? He . . . Good heavens! Williams! He's at the altar . . . And it's to you that I owe . . . Oh, my lord, let me fall at your feet! The feelings you arouse in me prevail over all others today. . . ."

"No, no," said Granwell, perturbed, "I can't yet enjoy your gratitude. This is the last moment when it must wring blood from my heart; don't show it to me, Henrietta, it will be painful to me only one day longer. . . . Tomorrow I can savor it more at ease. . . . Let's hurry; let's not keep the man who adores you waiting any longer: he's burning to be united with you."

Henrietta stepped forward, in a state of great excitement and inner turmoil; she was scarcely able to breathe, and never had the roses of her cheeks been brighter. Animated by love and hope, the dear girl thought that

her happiness was about to reach its peak. They came
to the end of an enormous gallery that led to the chapel of the castle . . . Oh, merciful heaven, what a sight!
That holy place was hung with black, and on a kind
of bier, surrounded by lighted candles, lay Williams'
body, pierced by thirteen daggers which were still in
the bleeding wounds they had opened.

"Here's your lover, you treacherous woman!" said
Granwell. "This is how my vengeance offers him to your
ignoble vows!"

"Traitor!" cried Henrietta, calling on all her strength
to prevent herself from fainting at this terrible moment.
"Ah, you told me the truth: every extreme of crime
must belong to your ferocious soul! Only virtue in it
would have surprised me. Let me die here, you heartless
monster, that's the last favor I ask of you."

"You won't obtain it yet," Granwell said with that
cold firmness which is common to all great villains. "My
vengeance is only half fulfilled; I must satisfy the rest.
Here's the altar that will receive our vows. It's here
that I want to hear you swear that you'll belong to me
forever."

Granwell insisted on being obeyed. Henrietta, courageous enough to withstand this crisis, felt her resolution fortified by her own desire for vengeance. She
promised everything and held back her tears.

"Henrietta," said Granwell when she had satisfied
him with her answers, "believe what I'm going to tell
you: my thirst for revenge is now entirely quenched,
and my only concern is to make up for my crimes.
Come with me, let's leave this gloomy scene. Everything is awaiting us in the temple: the public and the
ministers of heaven have long since arrived there before
us. Come and receive my hand there without delay. . . .

You'll devote tonight to the first duties of a wife, then tomorrow I shall publicly take you back to London and return you to your mother as my wife."

She looked at him with a distraught expression. She felt sure that she was not mistaken this time, but her stricken heart could no longer be consoled. Torn by despair and gnawed by her desire for vengeance, she was no longer capable of listening to any other feelings.

"My lord," she said with courageous calm, "I have such great confidence in your unexpected change of heart that I'm ready to grant you with good grace what you could take by force. Although our union hasn't yet been consecrated by heaven, I'm willing to fulfill its duties tonight, as you demand, so I beg you to put off the ceremony until we're back in London: it would upset me to have it without my mother's presence. It will make no difference to you, because I'm going to submit to all your desires in any case."

Although Granwell had really wanted to marry her, he saw with a kind of malicious joy that she was again willing to be taken in by him. Foreseeing that after a night of pleasure he might no longer be so scrupulous, he gladly consented to what she had asked of him.

Everything was calm for the rest of the day. Even the funereal decoration in the chapel was left unchanged, for it was essential that the darkest shadows of night should preside over poor Williams' burial.

"My lord," said Henrietta when she was about to retire, "I have another favor to beg of you. After what happened this morning, would it be possible for me to prevent myself from shuddering when I saw myself in the arms of my fiancé's murderer? Let the bed on which you will receive my troth be plunged in total darkness.

Don't you owe that consideration to my modesty? And haven't I suffered enough to acquire the right to obtain what I implore?"

"You have only to give me your orders," replied Granwell. "I should have to be extremely unjust to refuse you such a thing. I understand all too well the violence you'll have to do to yourself, and I give my wholehearted consent to anything that can diminish it."

Henrietta bowed and went to her room while Granwell, delighted with his infamous success, silently congratulated himself on having triumphed over his rival at last. He went to bed and the candles were taken from the room. Henrietta was notified that her wishes had been complied with and that she could come into the nuptial chamber whenever she wished.

When she came in she was armed with a dagger which she herself had pulled from her beloved's heart. She approached . . . On the pretext of guiding her steps, she took hold of Granwell with one hand, then with the other she plunged the dagger into him. The scoundrel fell to the floor, blaspheming against heaven and cursing the hand that had struck him down.

Henrietta immediately left the room and went to the funereal place where Williams' body lay. In one hand she held a lamp, in the other the bloody dagger which had just served her vengeance.

"Williams," she said, "crime has separated us, but the hand of God will bring us together again. Receive my soul, you whom I adored all my life; it will merge into yours and never be parted from it again. . . ."

With these words she stabbed herself and fell quivering upon that cold body. In an involuntary movement, her lips pressed her last kisses on it.

News of these appalling events soon reached London. Granwell was little missed there: his wrongdoing had long since made him odious. Gave, afraid of becoming involved in those terrible happenings, immediately went to Italy, and the grief-stricken Lady Stralson returned alone to Hereford, where she never ceased mourning her double loss until God, touched by her tears, deigned to call her back into His bosom and reunite her, in a better world, with those loved ones who were so worthy of her love, and who had been taken from her by licentiousness, vengeance, cruelty and all the other crimes that arise from the abuse of wealth and influence, and, above all, from disregard of those honorable principles without which neither we nor those around us can be happy on this earth.

Florville and Courval

or

Fatalism

Monsieur de Courval had just turned fifty-five. Vigorous and healthy, he could reasonably expect to live another twenty years. Having had nothing but unpleasantness from his first wife, who had long ago abandoned him in order to throw herself into a life of debauchery, and being obliged, on the basis of unequivocal testimony, to assume that this creature was in her grave, he began contemplating the idea of again entering into the bonds of matrimony, this time with a sensible woman who, by the kindness of her character and the excellence of her morals, would make him forget his earlier mishaps.

Unfortunate in his children as well as in his wife, he had had only two: a girl whom he had lost at a very early age, and a boy who, at the age of fifteen, had abandoned him as his wife had done, unfortunately in order to pursue the same licentious ways. Believing that nothing would ever bind him to this monster, Monsieur de Courval planned to disinherit him and bequeath all his possessions to the children he hoped to have with the new wife he wanted to take. He had an income of fifteen thousand francs a year; he had formerly been in business, and this was the fruit of his work. He was living on it in a respectable manner, with a few friends who all cherished and esteemed him, and saw him either in Paris, where he had an attractive apartment on the Rue Saint-Marc, or, more often, on a charming little estate near Nemours, where he spent two-thirds of the year.

This upright man confided his plan to his friends. When they expressed approval of it, he urged them to ask among their acquaintances to learn whether any of them knew a woman between the ages of thirty and thirty-five, either unmarried or a widow, who might fulfill his wishes.

Two days later one of his former colleagues came to tell him that he thought he had found exactly what he needed.

"The girl I'm proposing to you," this friend said to him, "has two things against her; I'll begin by telling them to you, so that I can console you afterward by describing her good qualities. It's certain that her parents are not alive, but no one knows who they were or where she lost them. All that's known is that she's a cousin of Monsieur de Saint-Prât, a reputable man who acknowledges her, holds her in great esteem, and will gladly express to you his enthusiastic and well-deserved praise of her. She has no inheritance from her parents, but Monsieur de Saint-Prât gives her four thousand francs a year. She was brought up in his house and spent her whole youth there. So much for her first fault, let's go on to her second: an affair at the age of sixteen, and a child who's no longer alive. She's never seen the father again. Those are the things against her; now for a few words about those in her favor.

"Mademoiselle de Florville is thirty-six, but she looks no more than twenty-eight. It would be difficult to imagine a more pleasing and interesting face. Her features are soft and delicate, her skin has the whiteness of a lily, and her brown hair hangs down almost to her feet. Her fresh, appealing mouth is like a springtime rose. She's very tall, but she has such an excellent figure, and so much grace in her movements, that no one is unfavorably impressed by her height, which might otherwise give her a rather hard appearance. Her arms, her neck and her legs are all shapely, and she has a kind of beauty that will not grow old for a long time.

"As for her conduct, its extreme regularity may not please you. She doesn't like social activities, and she leads a secluded life. She's very pious and very conscientious in the duties of the convent in which she lives. While she edifies everyone around her by religious qualities, she also enchants everyone who sees her by the charms of her mind and the sweetness of her character. . . . In short, she's an angel on earth, sent by heaven for the happiness of your old age."

Monsieur de Courval, delighted by this description, eagerly asked his friend to let him see the girl in question.

"I don't care about her birth," he said. "As long as her blood is pure, what does it matter who transmitted it to her? And her adventure at the age of sixteen doesn't alarm me, either: she's made up for that failing by many years of virtuous conduct. I'll simply consider that I'm marrying a widow; having decided to take a woman between thirty and thirty-five, it would have been hard for me to maintain a foolish insistence on virginity. So nothing displeases me in your proposal, and I can only urge you to let me see the object of it."

Monsieur de Courval's friend soon granted his wish: three days later he invited him to dinner with the young woman of whom he had spoken. It would have been difficult not to be enchanted at first sight by that charming girl. She had the features of Minerva herself, disguised beneath those of love. Since she knew what was at issue, she was even more reserved than usual. Her discretion, her modesty and the nobility of her bearing, combined with her many physical charms, her gentle character and her keen, well-developed mind, left poor Courval so enraptured that he begged his friend to hasten the conclusion.

He saw her several more times, in his friend's house, in his own, and in Monsieur de Saint-Prât's. Finally, in response to his earnest entreaties, she told him that nothing could be more pleasing to her than the honor he wanted to bestow on her, but that her conscience would not allow her to accept it until she herself had related the vicissitudes of her life to him.

"You haven't been told everything, monsieur," she said, "and I can't consent to be yours unless you know more about me. Your esteem is so important to me that I don't want to risk losing it, and I would certainly not deserve it if, taking advantage of your illusions about me, I were to agree to be your wife without giving you a chance to judge whether or not I'm worthy of it."

Monsieur de Courval assured her that he knew everything, that it was he, rather than she, who ought to have misgivings about his worthiness, and that if he was fortunate enough to please her, she had no reason to trouble herself about anything. But she held firm: she told him emphatically that she would not consent to anything until he had been thoroughly informed by her. He had to give in to her; all he was able to obtain from her was that she would come to his estate near Nemours, that all preparations would be made for the wedding he desired, and that she would become his wife the day after he had heard her story.

"But, monsieur," said that gracious girl, "since all those preparations may be in vain, why make them?

What if I should persuade you that I'm not meant for you?"

"You'll never prove that to me, mademoiselle," replied the honest Courval. "I defy you to prove it to me. Let us go, I beg you, and don't oppose my plans."

It was impossible to make him change his mind. Everything was arranged and they went to his estate. They were alone, however, as Mademoiselle de Florville had demanded: the things she had to say were not to be revealed to anyone except the man who wanted to marry her, so no one else was admitted. The day after their arrival, that beautiful and interesting girl asked Monsieur de Courval to listen to her, and told him the events of her life in these words:

Mademoiselle de Florville's Story

Your intentions with regard to me, monsieur, make it imperative that you be deceived no longer. You've seen Monsieur de Saint-Prât; you've been told that I'm related to him, and he himself was kind enough to say so, and yet you were greatly deceived on that point. My family is unknown to me; I've never had the satisfaction of knowing to whom I owe my birth. A few days after I was born, I was found in a green taffeta bassinet on Monsieur de Saint-Prât's doorstep. Attached to the canopy over my bassinet was an anonymous letter which said simply:

> *Since you have been married for ten years without having a child and still want one every day, adopt this one. Her blood is pure: she is the fruit of a virtuous marriage, and not of debauchery; she comes from an honorable family. If she*

*does not please you, you can have her taken to
a foundling home. Do not make any inquiries,
because none of them would be successful. It is
impossible to tell you anything more.*

I was immediately taken in by the good people at
whose house I'd been left. They brought me up, took the
best possible care of me, and I can say that I owe them
everything. Since there was no indication of my name,
it pleased Madame de Saint-Prât to name me Florville.

I had just reached the age of fifteen when I had
the misfortune of seeing my foster mother die. Nothing
could express the grief I felt at losing her. I had become
so dear to her that just before her death she begged her
husband to allot me an income of four thousand francs
a year and never to abandon me. Monsieur de Saint-Prât
granted these two requests. He was also kind enough to
acknowledge me as a cousin of his wife and to draw
up a marriage contract for me under that title, as you
have seen.

He made it clear to me, however, that I could
no longer stay in his house. "I'm a widower, and still
young," that virtuous man said to me. "If you and I
were to live under the same roof now, it would give
rise to doubts which we don't deserve. Your happiness
and your reputation are dear to me; I don't want to
endanger either of them. We must part, Florville, but
I will never abandon you as long as I live, and I don't
even want you to go outside of my family. I have a
widowed sister in Nancy. I'm going to send you to her.
You can count on her friendship the same as mine. With
her, you'll still be before my eyes, so to speak, and I can
continue to take care of everything that will be required
to complete your education and establish you in life."

I wept when I heard this news. It gave me an additional sorrow which bitterly renewed my grief over the death of my foster mother. But I was convinced of the soundness of Monsieur de Saint-Prât's reasoning, so I decided to follow his advice. I left for Lorraine in the company of a lady from that region to whom I had been entrusted. She brought me to Madame de Verquin, Monsieur de Saint-Prât's sister, with whom I was to live.

Madame de Verquin's house was quite different from Monsieur de Saint-Prât's. In his, I had seen decency, religion and morality reign supreme; in hers, frivolity, independence and the pursuit of pleasure were enthroned.

When I'd been there only a few days, Madame de Verquin warned me that my prudish air displeased her, that it was outrageous to come from Paris with such awkward manners and such a ridiculous strain of virtue in one's character, and that if I wanted to get along with her I'd have to adopt another tone. This beginning alarmed me. I won't try to make myself appear better than I am, monsieur, but everything contrary to morality and religion has always displeased me so intensely, I've always been so strongly opposed to anything that offends virtue, and the sins to which I've been driven in spite of myself have caused me so much remorse, that I must confess to you that you won't be rendering me a service if you bring me back into the world. I wasn't made to live in it, it makes me feel shy and morose. The deepest seclusion is what best suits the state of my soul and the inclinations of my mind.

These reflections, still badly formulated and not sufficiently ripened at such an early age, saved me neither from Madame de Verquin's bad advice nor from the calamities into which her enticement was to plunge me. The constant company and hectic pleasures with which I was surrounded, the examples and words of others—everything combined to lead me astray. I was told that I was pretty, and, unfortunately for me, I dared to believe it.

The Normandy regiment was garrisoned in Nancy at that time. Madame de Verquin's house was a meeting place for the officers. All the young women came too, and it was there that all the amorous intrigues of the town were begun, broken off and recomposed.

It was unlikely that Monsieur de Saint-Prât knew all about his sister's conduct. With his austere morality, how could he have consented to send me to her if he had known her well? This consideration held me back and prevented me from complaining to him. And, if I must confess everything, it's even possible that I had little desire to complain to him. The impure air I was breathing had begun to pollute my soul, and, like Telemachus on Calypso's island, I might not have listened to Mentor's advice.

One day the shameless Madame de Verquin, who had been trying to corrupt me for a long time, asked me whether I was sure I'd brought a pure heart with me to Lorraine, and whether I hadn't left a lover behind me in Paris.

"I've never even thought of the failings you suspect me of," I replied, "and your brother will answer for my conduct . . ."

"Failings?" interrupted Madame de Verquin. "If you have one, it's being too innocent for your age. I hope you'll correct it."

"Oh, madame! Is that the kind of language I ought to hear from such a respectable lady?"

"Respectable? Ah, not another word! I assure you, my dear, that respect is the feeling I care least about. Love is what I want to inspire. I'm not yet old enough for respect. Follow my example, my dear, and you'll be happy . . . By the way, have you noticed Senneval?" added that siren, referring to a seventeen-year-old officer who often came to her house.

"Not particularly," I replied. "I can assure you that I see them all with the same indifference."

"That's just what you mustn't do, my young friend. From now on, I want us to share our conquests. You must have Senneval. He's my handiwork, I've taken the trouble to develop him. He's in love with you. You must have him . . ."

"Oh, madame, please don't insist on it! Really, I'm not interested in anyone!"

"You must do it: I've already made arrangements with his colonel, who's my current lover, as you've seen."

"Please leave me free to make my own choice. I'm not at all inclined toward the pleasures you cherish."

"Oh, that will change! Some day you'll like them as much as I do. It's easy not to cherish something you don't know yet, but it's inadmissible to refuse to know something that was made to be adored. In short, the whole thing has already been planned: Senneval will declare his passion to you this evening, and I don't want you to make him wait too long before you satisfy it, otherwise I'll be angry with you—seriously angry."

At five o'clock the company gathered. Since the weather was hot, card games were organized outside in the groves. Things had been so well arranged that Monsieur de Senneval and I found that we were the only ones who were not playing cards, so we were obliged to talk with each other.

It would be pointless to conceal the fact that as soon as that charming and witty young man had told me of his love for me, I felt irresistibly drawn toward him. When I later tried to understand that attraction, I found that everything about it was obscure to me. It seemed to me that it wasn't the effect of an ordinary feeling; its characteristics were hidden from me by a veil before my eyes. On the other hand, at the very moment when my heart flew toward him, an invincible force seemed to hold it back, and in that tumult, that ebb and flow of incomprehensible ideas, I was unable to decide whether I was right to love Senneval or whether I ought to flee from him forever.

He was given ample time to confess his love to me . . . Alas, he was given too much! I had time enough to appear responsive to him. Taking advantage of my agitation, he demanded an admission of my feelings. I was weak enough to tell him that he was far from displeasing me, and three days later I was sinful enough to let him enjoy his victory.

The malicious joy of vice in its triumphs over virtue is a truly extraordinary thing. Madame de Verquin was ecstatic when she learned that I'd fallen into the trap she'd set for me. She made fun of me, laughed at me, and finally assured me that what I'd done was the simplest, most reasonable thing in the world, and that I could receive my lover in her house every night without fear, because she would see nothing. She said she was too busy to concern herself with such trifles, but that she would admire my virtue nevertheless, because I would probably limit myself to the one lover I had just chosen, while she, lacking my modesty and reserve, had to contend with three of them at once.

When I took the liberty of telling her that such promiscuity was odious, that it presupposed neither sensitivity nor sentiment, and that it reduced our sex to the level of the vilest species of animals, she burst out laughing and said, " 'Gallic heroine,' I admire you and don't blame you. I know very well that at your age sensitivity and sentiment are gods to whom one sacrifices pleasure. At my age, it's different: completely disillusioned about those phantoms, one gives them a little less power; sensual pleasures that are more real are preferred to the silly delusions that fill you with enthusiasm. Why should we be faithful to men who aren't faithful to us? Isn't it enough to be weaker without also being more gullible? A woman who has any qualms about such actions is foolish. . . . Take my advice, my dear: vary your pleasures while your age and your charms allow you to do it, and abandon your absurd faithfulness. It's a gloomy, repugnant virtue that's unsatisfying in itself and never impresses others."

These words made me shudder, but I saw clearly that I no longer had the right to oppose them; the criminal co-operation of that immoral woman had become necessary to me, and I had to treat her with consideration. This is one of the fatal disadvantages of vice: as soon as we abandon ourselves to it, it places us in bondage to people whom we would otherwise scorn. And so I accepted all of Madame de Verquin's obligingness. Every night Senneval gave me new proof of his love, and I spent the next six months in such a passionate turmoil that I scarcely had time to think.

My eyes were opened by a disastrous consequence: I became pregnant. I nearly died of despair when I discovered my condition. Madame de Verquin was amused by it. "However," she said, "we must save appearances. Since it wouldn't be very decent for you to have your baby in my house, Senneval's colonel and I have made some arrangements. He's going to give Senneval a leave. You'll go to Metz, he'll join you there a few days later, and then, with his aid, you'll give birth to the illicit fruit of your love. Afterward, you'll both come back here, one after the other, the same as you'll have left."

I had to obey. As I've already said, monsieur, we place ourselves at the mercy of all men and all situations when we've been unfortunate enough to sink into sin; we give rights over ourselves to everyone in the world, we become the slaves of every living being as soon as we forget ourselves to the point of becoming the slaves of our passions.

Everything took place as Madame de Verquin had said. On the third day, Senneval and I were in Metz together, in the house of a midwife whose address I'd been given before I left Nancy, and there I gave birth to a boy. Senneval, who had never stopped showing the most tender and delicate feelings for me, seemed to love me even more as soon as I had doubled his existence, as he put it. He was full of consideration for me; he begged me to leave his son to him, swore that he would take all possible care of him for the rest of his life, and wouldn't think of returning to Nancy until he had fulfilled his obligations to me.

It was not until he was about to leave that I dared to point out to him how unhappy I was going to be because of the sin he had made me commit, and to suggest that we atone for it by consecrating our union before the altar. Senneval, who hadn't expected this, became upset.

"Alas," he said, "it's not within my power. I'm still a minor, so I'd have to have my father's consent. What would our marriage be without it? Besides, I'm by no means a good match for you. As Madame de Verquin's niece" (this was what everyone in Nancy believed) "you can expect something better. Believe me, Florville, the best thing we can do is to forget our mistakes. You can count on my discretion."

These words came as a shock to me, and they made me painfully aware of the enormity of my sin. My pride prevented me from replying, but my grief was all the more bitter. If anything had hidden the horror of my conduct from me, it was, I confess, the hope of making amends for it some day by marrying my lover. What a credulous girl I was! Although I should no doubt have been enlightened by Madame de Verquin's perversity, I hadn't believed that a man could amuse himself by seducing an unfortunate girl and then abandoning her, that the sentiment of honor, so highly respected among men, could be totally inoperative with regard to us, and that our weakness could justify an insult which one man could not inflict on another without risking his life. I saw that I was both the victim and the dupe of the man for whom I would gladly have given my life. This terrible realization nearly put me into my grave. Senneval didn't leave me; he took care of me the same as before, but he never spoke of my suggestion again, and I had too much pride to mention the cause of my despair to him a second time. He went away as soon as he saw that I'd recovered.

Determined never to go back to Nancy, and realizing that I was seeing my lover for the last time in my life, I felt all my wounds reopening when I said good-by to him. But I had the strength to withstand that final blow . . .

How cruel he was! He left, he tore himself away from my bosom wet with my tears, without shedding a single tear of his own!

Such is the result of the vows of love we're foolish enough to believe! The more sensitive we are, the more completely our seducers forsake us. . . . The traitors! The degree to which they abandon us is in proportion to our efforts to keep them with us.

Senneval had taken his child and placed him in a country home where it was impossible for me to find him. He wanted to deprive me of the sweet consolation of cherishing and bringing up that tender fruit of our union. It was as though he wanted me to forget everything that might still bind us to each other, and I did, or rather I thought I did.

I decided to leave Metz immediately and not go back to Nancy. I didn't want to quarrel with Madame de Verquin, however. Despite her faults, the fact that she was so closely related to my benefactor was enough to make me treat her with consideration all my life. I wrote to her in the most courteous possible terms, giving my shame over what I'd done in Nancy as my reason for not wanting to return there, and asking her to give me her permission to go back to her brother in Paris. She replied promptly that I was free to do as I pleased, and that I could always count on her friendship. She added that Senneval had not yet returned, that no one knew where he was, and that I was a fool to be so distressed by such trifles.

As soon as I received this letter I went back to Paris and hurried to throw myself at Monsieur de Saint-Prât's feet. My silence and my tears soon informed him of my unhappiness. But I was careful to accuse only myself: I never told him of his sister's deliberate efforts to lead me astray. With his kind, trusting nature, he had never suspected her disorderly life, and believed her to be the most respectable of women. I did nothing to destroy his illusion, and this conduct on my part, which Madame de Verquin knew about, preserved her friendship for me.

Monsieur de Saint-Prât pitied me, made me even more keenly aware of the wrong I'd done, and finally forgave me for it.

"Ah, my child," he said with the gentle gravity of an honorable soul, so different from the odious delirium of crime, "my dear daughter, now you know what it costs to forsake virtue. . . . Its practice is so necessary and so intimately bound up with our existence that there's nothing but unhappiness for us as soon as we abandon it. Compare the tranquillity of the state of innocence in which you left this house to the terrible turmoil in which you've returned to it. Do the weak pleasures you savored during your downfall compensate for the torments that now rend your heart? Happiness lies only in virtue, my child, and all the sophisms of its detractors will never bring us a single one of its enjoyments. Ah, Florville, you may be sure that those who deny or oppose those sweet enjoyments do so only out of jealousy, for the barbarous pleasure of making others as guilty and unhappy as themselves. They've blinded themselves and want to blind everyone else; they're mistaken and they want everyone else to be mistaken. But if one could see into the depths of their souls, one would find only sorrow and remorse: all those apostles of crime are full of wretchedness and despair. There's not one of them who, if he were sincere, if he could tell the truth, wouldn't admit that his foul words or his dangerous writings had been guided only by his passions. And who can seriously maintain that the foundations of morality can be shaken without risk? Who would dare to say that doing and desiring good must not necessarily be man's purpose? And how can someone who does only evil expect to be happy in a society whose most powerful interest is that good should be constantly multiplied? But will not even that apologist of crime shudder when he has uprooted from every heart the only thing from which he can expect his preservation? Who will restrain his servants from ruining him if they have ceased to be virtuous? Who will prevent his wife from dishonoring him if he has convinced her that virtue is useless? Who will hold back the hands of his children if he has dared to wither the seeds of good in their hearts? How will his freedom and his possessions be respected if he has said to the powerful, 'Impunity goes with you, and virtue is only an illusion'? No matter what that unhappy man's condition, whether he be a husband or a father, rich or poor, a master or a slave, dangers will spring up on all sides of him, and daggers will be raised above his heart from all directions. If he has dared to destroy in man the only duties which balance his perversity, you may be sure that the poor wretch will perish sooner or later, the victim of his own horrible systems.*

"Let us leave religion for the moment and, if you like, let us consider man alone. Who would be stupid

---

*"Ah, my friend, never try to corrupt the person you love: it may go further than you think!" said a sensitive woman one day to a friend who was trying to seduce her. Adorable woman, let me quote your remark; it depicts so well the soul of the woman who saved that same man's life a short time later that I would like to engrave those touching words in the temple of memory, where your virtues assure you of a place.

enough to think that if he breaks all the laws of society, that society which he has outraged can leave him in peace? Is it not in the interest of man, and the laws he has made for his safety, always to try to destroy whatever is obstructive or harmful? A certain amount of influence or wealth may give the wicked man a fleeting glow of well-being, but how short its duration will be! He will soon be recognized, unmasked and made an object of public hatred and contempt. Will he then find the apologists of his conduct? Will his partisans come forward to console him? None of them will acknowledge him. Now that he no longer has everything to offer them, they will all cast him off like a burden. Misfortune will surround him, he will languish in disgrace and sorrow, and, no longer having even his own heart as a refuge, he will soon die in despair.

"What, then, is this absurd reasoning of our adversaries? What is this impotent effort to diminish virtue, to dare to say that anything which is not universal is illusory, and that since virtues are only local, none of them can have any reality? What! Is there no virtue because each people has had to make its own? If different climates and different kinds of temperament have made different kinds of restraints necessary, if, in a word, virtue has multiplied in a thousand forms, does this mean that there is no virtue on earth? One might as well doubt the reality of a river because it splits off into a thousand different streams. What better proof of the existence and necessity of virtue is there than man's need to adapt it to all his different moral codes and to make it the basis of all of them?

"If anyone can find me a single people which lives without virtue, a single one for which benevolence and kindness are not fundamental bonds . . . I will go further: if anyone can show me even an association of criminals which is not held together by a few principles of virtue, then I will abandon its cause. But if, on the contrary, it can be demonstrated to be useful everywhere, if there is no nation, class, group or individual that can do without it, if no man, in short, can live either happily or safely without it, then, my child, am I wrong to urge you never to depart from it?

"You see where your first lapse has led you, Florville!" continued my benefactor, clasping me in his arms. "If error should solicit you again, if seduction or your weakness should set new traps for you, remember the misery of this first lapse, think of the man who loves you as though you were his own daughter and whose heart is torn by your failings, and you will find in these reflections all the strength required by devotion to virtue, which I want to instill in you forever."

In accordance with these same principles, Monsieur de Saint-Prât didn't offer to let me stay in his house, but he suggested that I go and live with one of his relatives, a woman as famous for the lofty piety of her life as Madame de Verquin was for her immorality. This arrangement pleased me greatly. Madame de Lérince accepted me gladly, and I was installed in her house less than a week after my return to Paris.

Ah, monsieur, what a difference between that respectable woman and the woman I had just left! If vice and depravity had established their dominion in Madame de Verquin, it was as though Madame de Lérince's heart had become the sanctuary of all the virtues. I had been frightened by Madame de Verquin's depravity; I was consoled by Madame de Lérince's edifying principles. I had found only bitterness and remorse in listening to Madame de Verquin; I found only sweetness and consolations in abandoning myself to Madame de Lérince . . . Ah, monsieur, let me describe that adorable woman whom I shall always love! It's a tribute that my heart owes to her virtues, and it's impossible for me to resist it.

Madame de Lérince was about forty years old; she still had the bloom of youth, and her air of candor and modesty did much more to make her face beautiful than the divine proportions that nature had given to her features. Some of those who knew her thought that a little too much nobility and majesty made her rather awesome at first sight, but what might have been taken for pride became softened as soon as she spoke. She had such a pure and beautiful soul, such perfect graciousness and such complete frankness that, in spite of oneself, one always became aware of tender feelings gradually arising beside the veneration she inspired at first.

There was nothing exaggerated or superstitious in Madame de Lérince's religion. The principles of her faith resided in an extreme sensibility. The idea of the existence of God, the worship owed to that Supreme Being: such were the keenest enjoyments of that loving soul. She avowed openly that she would be the most wretched of creatures if some sort of perfidious enlightenment should ever force her mind to destroy in her the respect and love she had for her religion.

Still more strongly attached, if possible, to the sublime morality of her religion than to its practices and ceremonies, she made that excellent morality the rule of all her actions. Slander never soiled her lips; she would not tolerate even a jest which might hurt someone's feelings. Full of affection and compassion for others, finding them interesting even in their faults, she was solely concerned with either carefully hiding those faults or gently admonishing them. If others were unhappy, nothing was as gratifying to her as relieving their unhappiness. She didn't wait for the poor to come and implore her aid: she sought them out, she sensed their distress before they expressed it, and joy could be seen shining from her face when she had consoled a widow or provided for an orphan, when she had brought prosperity to a poor family, or when her hands had broken the chains of adversity. And there was nothing harsh or austere with all this: if the pleasures proposed to her were pure, she indulged in them with delight. She even invented pleasures herself, for fear others might be bored in her company.

Wise and enlightened with the moralist, profound with the theologian, she inspired the novelist and smiled on the poet, she astonished the legislator and the statesman, and directed the games of a child. She had every kind of intelligence, but the kind that shone most brightly in her was recognized chiefly by her special care and charming attention in bringing out the intelligence of others or expressing appreciation of it. Living in retirement by inclination, cultivating her friends for their own sake, Madame de Lérince, who could have served as a model for either sex, made all those around her enjoy the peaceful happiness and heavenly delight which is promised to the honest man by the holy God whose image she was.

I won't bore you, monsieur, with the monotonous details of my life during the seventeen years I was fortunate enough to live with that adorable woman. Discussions of morality and piety, as many benevolent acts as it was possible for us to perform: such were the duties that filled our days.

"People are frightened away from religion, my dear Florville," Madame de Lérince once said to me, "only because awkward guides point out nothing but its restraints to them, without offering them its sweetness. Can there be a man absurd enough to open his eyes to the universe and still dare not to agree that such wonders could only be the work of an all-powerful God? Once this first truth has been realized—and does one require anything more than one's heart in order to become convinced of it?—how can anyone be so cruel and barbarous as to refuse his homage to the benevolent God who created him?

"But the diversity of religions is cited as an objection: their falsity is thought to be proved by their multitude. What sophistry! Is not the existence of a supreme God proved more irrefutably by this unanimity of all peoples in recognizing and serving a God, and by this tacit avowal imprinted in the hearts of all men, than by the sublimities of nature? What! Man cannot live without adopting a God, he cannot question himself without finding evidence of Him within himself, he cannot open his eyes without seeing traces of Him everywhere, and yet he dares to doubt His existence!

"No, Florville, there are no atheists in good faith. Pride, stubbornness, the passions: those are the destructive weapons of that God who constantly re-vivifies Himself in man's heart or reason. And when each beat of that heart and each bright ray of that reason offer me that incontestable Being, shall I refuse my homage to Him? Shall I rob Him of the tribute which His goodness allows my weakness? Shall I not humiliate myself before His greatness, and ask Him to help me endure the miseries of life and participate in His glory some day? Shall I not aspire to the favor of spending eternity in His bosom, or shall I risk spending that eternity in a frightful abyss of torments because I've refused to accept the indubitable proofs of that great Being's existence which He has been kind enough to give me? My child, does that appalling choice permit even a moment's reflection? Ah, you who stubbornly refuse to let yourselves recognize the letters of fire that God has traced in the depths of your hearts, be just for at least a moment, and, if only out of pity for yourselves, yield to this invincible argument of Pascal's: 'If there is no God, what does it matter to you if you believe in Him, what harm does it do you? And if there is a God, what risks will you be taking if you refuse Him your faith?'

"But you say, skeptics, that you don't know what tribute to pay to this God; you're repelled by the multitude of religions. Very well, examine them all, I have no objection; then afterward come and tell me sincerely in which one of them you find the most grandeur and majesty. Deny if you can, Christians, that the religion in which you were fortunate enough to be born is the one whose characteristics appear to you the holiest and most sublime; seek elsewhere such great mysteries, such pure dogmas, such consoling morality; find in another religion the ineffable sacrifice of a God in favor of His creature, see in it more beautiful promises, a more appealing future, a greater and more sublime God! No, you cannot, philosopher of the day; you cannot, slave of your pleasures whose faith changes with the physical state of your nerves, so that you are impious in the fire of the passions and a believer as soon as they are calmed; you cannot, I tell you. Sentiment constantly acknowledges the God your mind combats. He always exists beside you, even in the midst of your errors. Break the chains which bind you to crime and that holy and majestic God will never leave the temple He has built in your heart.

"It is in the depths of the heart, my dear Florville, even more than in the mind, that we must seek the necessity of that God whom everything indicates and proves to us. It is also from the heart that we must receive the necessity of the worship we devote to Him. And it is the heart alone, my dear friend, that will soon convince you that the noblest and purest of all religions is the one in which we were born. Let us therefore practice that sweet and consoling religion with exactitude and joy. May it fill our most beautiful moments in this world, may we cherish it until we are gradually led to the end of our life, and may it be by a path of love and delights that we go to place in the bosom of God that soul which emanated from Him, which was formed solely to know Him, and which we should have enjoyed only to believe in Him and worship Him."

That's how Madame de Lérince spoke to me, that's how my mind was strengthened by her advice, and how my soul was refined beneath her holy wing. But, as I've told you, I'm going to pass in silence over the little details of my life in that house and dwell only on what's essential. It's my sins that I must reveal to you, generous and sensitive man, and when heaven has allowed me to live peacefully in the path of virtue, I have only to be thankful and remain silent.

I continued to write to Madame de Verquin. I heard from her regularly twice a month. I should no doubt have stopped writing to her, and I was more or less obliged to do so by my better principles and the reformation of my life, but what I owed to Monsieur de Saint-Prât, the hope of perhaps receiving news of my son some day, and, most of all, I must confess, a secret feeling which still drew me toward the place to which cherished people had bound me in the past—all these things made me inclined to continue our correspondence, which she was courteous enough to maintain regularly. I tried to convert her, I praised the sweetness of the life I was leading, but she called it an illusion. She never stopped making fun of my resolutions or combating them, and, still firm in her own, she assured me that nothing in the world could weaken them. She told me of the new girls she had converted to her principles for her own amusement, and she claimed that their docility was much greater than mine. Their multiple lapses from virtue, said that perverse woman, were little triumphs which she was always delighted to win, and the pleasure of leading those young hearts into evil consoled her for not being able to do as much of it as her imagination dictated to her.

I often asked Madame de Lérince to lend me her eloquent pen in order to overthrow my adversary, and she was glad to do so. Madame de Verquin replied to us; her sophisms, sometimes very powerful, forced us to resort to the more victorious arguments of a sensitive soul, in which was inevitably found, Madame de Lérince rightly claimed, everything that could destroy vice and confound unbelief.

I occasionally asked Madame de Verquin for news of the man I still loved, but she was always either unwilling or unable to give me any.

The time has come, monsieur; I must tell you of the second catastrophe of my life, the cruel event that breaks my heart each time it presents itself to my imagination. When you have heard it and learned from it the horrible crime of which I am guilty, you will no doubt give up the flattering plans you made with regard to me.

Although Madame de Lérince's house was as orderly as I've described it to you, she nevertheless opened it to a few friends. One day Madame de Dulfort, a middle-aged lady who had once belonged to the household of the Princess of Piedmont, and who came to see us very often, asked Madame de Lérince for permission to introduce to her a young man who had been expressly recommended to her, and whom she would be glad to bring into a house where the examples of virtue he would constantly receive could not fail to contribute to forming his heart. My protectress apologized at first, saying that she never received young men; then, vanquished by her friend's earnest entreaties, she consented to see the Chevalier de Saint-Ange.

He appeared. Whether from a presentiment or any other reason you may care to name, monsieur, as soon as I saw that young man I began to quiver all over without being able to determine the cause. I was on the verge of fainting. . . . Not seeking the reason for that strange reaction, I attributed it to some inner indisposition, and Saint-Ange stopped troubling me.

But while he had agitated me at first sight, a similar reaction had also taken place in him, as he later told me himself. He was filled with such great veneration for the house into which he had been admitted that he didn't dare to forget himself to the point of revealing the flame that was consuming him. And so three months went by before he ventured to say anything about it to me; but his eyes expressed his feelings so vividly that it was impossible for me to mistake their meaning. Determined not to relapse into a sin which had caused the greatest unhappiness of my life, and strengthened now by better principles, I was ready a score of times to inform Madame de Lérince of the feelings I thought I discerned in Saint-Ange; but at the last moment I was always held back by the alarm I was afraid of causing her, and so I said nothing. This was undoubtedly the wrong decision, for it was the cause of the frightful disaster I will soon relate to you.

We were in the habit of spending six months of every year in Madame de Lérince's attractive country house five miles outside of Paris. Monsieur de Saint-Prât often came to see us there. Unfortunately for me, he had an attack of gout that year and was unable to come. I say "unfortunately for me," monsieur, because, having naturally more confidence in him than in Madame de Lérince, I would have told him things I was never able to bring myself to tell anyone else, and telling them to him would no doubt have prevented the deadly accident that happened.

Saint-Ange asked Madame de Lérince for permission to come with us, and since Madame de Dulfort also requested this favor for him, it was granted.

Everyone in our group was rather uneasy about our lack of knowledge of this young man; nothing very clear or definite was known about his life. Madame de Dulfort had told us he was the son of a provincial gentleman to whom she was related. As for Saint-Ange himself, he sometimes forgot what Madame de Dulfort had said and referred to himself as Piedmontese, a claim which seemed rather well supported by the way he spoke Italian. Although he was old enough to do something in life, he hadn't yet embarked on any career and showed no inclination to do so. He had a very handsome face, worthy of an artist's brush. His manners were excellent, he always spoke courteously, and he gave every indication of being well bred; but through all this there was a prodigious intensity, a kind of impetuosity in his character which sometimes frightened us.

The curb he had tried to impose on his feelings had only made them grow. As soon as he was in Madame de Lérince's country house it became impossible for him to conceal them from me. I trembled . . . but I summoned up enough self-control to show him only pity.

"Really, monsieur," I said to him, "you must have a false idea of your own worth, or else you have time to waste, since you spend it with a woman twice your age. But even assuming that I should be foolish enough to listen to you, what ridiculous aims would you dare to form concerning me?"

"My only aim would be to bind myself to you by the holiest of ties, mademoiselle. How little respect you would have for me if you thought I had any other!"

"Let me assure you, monsieur, that I would never offer the public the strange spectacle of a woman of thirty-four marrying a boy of seventeen."

"Ah, cruel woman, would you be aware of that slight difference if your heart contained even a thousandth of the fire that's consuming mine?"

"It's certain, monsieur, that for my part I'm quite calm. I've been calm for many years, and I hope I shall continue for as long as it pleases God to let me languish on this earth."

"You deprive me of even the hope of moving you to pity some day."

"I go further: I dare to forbid you to speak to me of your madness any longer."

"Ah, fair Florville, do you want my life to be miserable?"

"I want it to be peaceful and happy."

"It can be neither without you."

"No, not until you've destroyed the ridiculous feelings you never should have conceived. Try to overcome them, try to control yourself, and your tranquillity will return."

"I can't."

"You don't want to. We must part before you can succeed. If you spend two years without seeing me, your agitation will pass, you'll forget me, and you'll be happy."

"Ah, never! Never shall I find happiness anywhere but at your feet. . . ."

Just then the others rejoined us, so our first conversation stopped at that point.

Three days later, Saint-Ange succeeded in being alone with me again and tried to resume our discussion in the same tone as before. This time I imposed silence on him so sternly that his tears flowed abundantly. He left me abruptly, after telling me that I was driving him to despair and that he would soon take his own life if I continued to treat him as I was doing. Then he turned around, hurried back to me like a madman and said, "Mademoiselle, you don't know the soul you're insulting! No, you don't know it. . . . Let me tell you that I'm capable of going to violent extremes . . . extremes that you may be far from thinking of. . . . Yes, I'll resort to them a thousand times rather than renounce the happiness of belonging to you." And he left in terrible grief.

I was never more strongly tempted to speak to Madame de Lérince than I was then, but, as I've already said, I was restrained by the fear of harming Saint-Ange. I said nothing. For a week he fled from me, scarcely speaking to me, avoiding me at table, in the drawing room, and during our walks. All this was no doubt done in order to see whether his change of conduct would make an impression on me. It would have been an effective means if I had shared his feelings, but I was so far from doing so that I hardly seemed to be aware of his maneuvers.

Finally he came up to me in the garden and said, in the most violent state imaginable, "Mademoiselle, I've at last succeeded in calming myself. Your advice has had the effect on me that you expected: you can see how tranquil I've become. I've tried to find you alone only because I want to tell you good-by.... Yes, I'm going away from you forever, mademoiselle, I'm going away.... You'll never again see the man you hate.... Oh, no, you'll never see him again!"

"I'm glad to hear of your plan, monsieur. I like to think that you've become reasonable at last. But," I added, smiling, "your conversion doesn't seem very real to me."

"Well, then, how should I be, mademoiselle, in order to convince you of my indifference?"

"Quite different from the way I see you now."

"But at least when I'm gone, when you no longer have the pain of seeing me, perhaps you'll believe that all your efforts have finally succeeded in making me reasonable."

"It's true that only your departure would convince me of it, and I'll continue to advise you to leave."

"Then I must be terribly repulsive to you!"

"You're a charming man, monsieur, who ought to pursue conquests of a different value and leave me in peace, because it's impossible for me to listen to you."

"But you *will* listen to me!" he said furiously. "Yes,

cruel woman, you'll listen, no matter what you say, to the feelings of my fiery soul, and to the assurance that there's nothing in the world I won't do either to deserve you or to obtain you. . . . And don't believe in my pretended departure," he went on impetuously. "I told you about it only to test you. . . . Do you really think I'd leave you? Do you think I could tear myself away from the place where you are? I'd rather die a thousand deaths! Hate me, traitress, hate me, since that's my unhappy fate, but never hope to overcome the love for you with which I'm burning. . . ."

When he spoke these last words he was in such a state that, by a mischance which I've never been able to understand, I was deeply moved and turned away from him to hide my tears. I left him in the thicket where he had joined me. He didn't follow me. I heard him throw himself on the ground and abandon himself to the excesses of a horrible delirium. . . . And I must admit to you, monsieur, that although I was quite certain of having no feeling of love for him, whether from commiseration or memory it was impossible for me not to give vent to my own emotion.

"Alas," I said to myself, yielding to my sorrow, "Senneval spoke to me in the same way! It was in the same terms that he expressed his passion to me. . . . And also in a garden, a garden like this one . . . He told me he would always love me, and yet he cruelly deceived me! Good heavens, he was the same age! . . . Ah, Senneval, Senneval, are you trying to take away my peace of mind again? Have you reappeared in this seductive guise to drag me into the abyss a second time? Away, coward, away! I now abhor even your memory!"

I wiped my eyes and stayed in my room till supper time. I then went downstairs. But Saint-Ange didn't appear, having announced that he was ill. And the next day he was adroit enough to let me see only serenity on his face. I was deceived by him: I really believed he had exercised enough self-control to overcome his passion. I was mistaken, the treacherous deceiver! ... Alas, what am I saying, monsieur? I no longer owe him invectives.... I owe him only my tears and my remorse.

He appeared so calm only because he had already made his plans. Two days went by like this, and toward the evening of the third he publicly announced his departure. He made arrangements with Madame de Dulfort, his protectress, concerning their common affairs in Paris.

We all went to bed ... Forgive me, monsieur, for the agitation which the story of that terrible catastrophe arouses in me in advance; it never presents itself to my memory without making me shudder with horror.

Since it was a very hot night, I lay down on my bed almost naked. As soon as my maid left, I put out my candle. A sewing bag had unfortunately remained open on my bed, because I'd just cut some gauze I was going to need the next day. My eyes had scarcely begun to close when I heard a sound.... I quickly sat up. I felt a hand seize me ...

"This time you won't get away from me, Florville," said Saint-Ange, for it was he. "Forgive the excessiveness of my passion, but don't try to escape from it. I must make you mine!"

"Infamous seducer!" I cried. "Get out immediately, or fear the effects of my anger!"

"I fear nothing except not being able to possess you, cruel girl!" said that ardent young man, throwing himself on me so skillfully and in such a state of frenzy that I became his victim before I was able to do anything to prevent it. . . .

Enraged by his audacity and determined to do anything rather than submit to it any further, I broke away from him and snatched up the scissors that were lying at my feet. But even in my fury I retained a certain amount of self-control: I sought his arm, intending to stab him in it, much more to frighten him by my resolution than to punish him as he deserved. When he felt my movements he redoubled the violence of his own.

"Traitor!" I cried, stabbing what I thought was his arm. "Get out this instant! And blush with shame for your crime!"

Oh, monsieur, a fatal hand had guided mine! The poor young man uttered a cry and fell to the floor. I quickly lit a candle and bent down over him. . . . Good heavens! I had stabbed him in the heart! He died. . . . I threw myself onto his bleeding body and feverishly clasped it to my agitated bosom. . . . I pressed my mouth to his, trying to bring back his departed soul. I washed his wound with my tears. . . .

"Ah, you whose only crime was to love me too much," I said in the frenzy of despair, "did you deserve such a death? Should you have died by the hand of the woman for whom you would have sacrificed your life? Unhappy young man, image of him whom I once adored, if all I must do is to love you in order to bring you back to life, let me tell you at this cruel moment when you can unfortunately no longer hear me, let me tell you, if your soul is still palpitating, that I wish I could revive you at the cost of my own life. . . . I want you to know that I was never indifferent to you, that I never saw you without emotion, and that my feelings for you were perhaps far superior to the weak love that burned in your heart."

With these words I fell unconscious onto the body of that unfortunate young man. My maid came in, having heard the sound of my fall. She brought me back to my senses, then she joined me in trying to revive Saint-Ange. Alas, all our efforts were in vain. We left that fateful room, carefully locked its door, took the key with us and immediately hurried to Monsieur de Saint-Prât's house in Paris. I had him awakened, gave him the key to that sinister chamber and told him my horrible story. He pitied me and consoled me, and then, even though he was ill, he went straight to Madame de Lérince's house. Since it was quite close to Paris, he arrived as everyone was getting up, before the events of the night had become known. Never have friends or relatives conducted themselves better. Far from imitating those stupid or ferocious people whose only concern in such crises is to make known everything that can bring dishonor or unhappiness to themselves and those around them, they acted in such a way that even the servants scarcely had any suspicion of what had occurred.

At this point, Mademoiselle de Florville broke off her narrative because of the tears that were choking her; then she said to Monsieur de Courval, "Well, monsieur, now will you marry a woman capable of such a murder? Will you hold in your arms a creature who deserves the full severity of the law, a wretched creature who is constantly tormented by her crime, and who has never had a peaceful night since that cruel moment? No, monsieur, there has never been a single night when my unfortunate victim hasn't presented himself to me covered with the blood I tore from his heart!"

"Be calm, mademoiselle, be calm, I beg you," said Monsieur de Courval, mingling his tears with hers. "With the sensitive soul you've been given by nature, I understand your remorse. But there's not even the shadow of a crime in that fatal event. It was a terrible misfortune, of course, but that's all. There was nothing premeditated in it, nothing heinous; your only desire was to ward off an odious attack. . . . In short, it was a murder committed by chance, in self-defense. Put your mind at rest, mademoiselle, I insist on it. . . . The sternest tribunal would do nothing except wipe your tears. Ah, how mistaken you were if you were afraid that such an event would make you lose the rights to my heart which your personal qualities have given you. No, no, fair Florville, far from dishonoring you, it enhances your virtues in my eyes, and only makes you worthier of a consoling hand that will make you forget your sorrows."

"Monsieur de Saint-Prât also said what you've been kind enough to tell me," said Mademoiselle de Florville, "but the reproaches of my conscience can't be stifled by the great kindness you've both shown me, and nothing will ever soothe its remorse. But it doesn't matter; let me go on, monsieur, because you must be apprehensive about the outcome of all this."

And Mademoiselle de Florville continued her story:

Madame de Dulfort was grief-stricken; aside from Saint-Ange's intrinsic attractiveness, he had been so specially recommended to her that she couldn't fail to lament his loss. But she saw the reasons for silence, she realized that a public scandal would only ruin me without bringing her protégé back to life, and she said nothing.

Madame de Lérince, despite the severity of her principles and the extreme propriety of her morals, behaved still better, if that's possible, because prudence and humanity are the distinctive characteristics of true piety. She began by telling her household that I had capriciously decided to go back to Paris during the night in order to enjoy the cool weather, that she had been informed of this whim on my part, and that she had no objection to it because she herself was planning to go to Paris that evening for supper. On this pretext, she sent all her servants there. As soon as she was alone with Monsieur de Saint-Prât and Madame de Dulfort, she sent for the parish priest. Madame de Lérince's pastor was as wise and enlightened as herself; he gave Madame de Dulfort an official attestation without raising any objections, and then, with two of his servants, he secretly buried the unfortunate victim of my fury.

When these precautions had been taken, everyone reappeared and took an oath of secrecy. Monsieur de Saint-Prât came to calm me by telling me about everything that had been done to make sure that my act would remain shrouded in oblivion. He seemed to want me to resume my life in Madame de Lérince's house as before. She was ready to receive me. I told him I couldn't bring myself to do it. He then advised me to seek diversion. Madame de Verquin, with whom I'd never ceased to be in correspondence, as I've already told you, monsieur, was still urging me to come and spend a few months with her. I discussed this idea with her brother, he approved of it, and a week later I went to Lorraine. But the memory of my crime pursued me everywhere and nothing was able to calm me.

I often awoke in the middle of the night, thinking

I could still hear poor Saint-Ange's moans and cries; I saw him bleeding at my feet, reproaching me for my barbarity, assuring me that the memory of my horrible act would hound me to the end of my days, and that I didn't know the heart I'd pierced.

One night I dreamed that Senneval—that wretched lover whom I hadn't forgotten, since he alone still drew me toward Nancy—showed me two corpses: that of Saint-Ange and that of a woman who was unknown to me.* He shed tears on both of them, and pointed to a nearby coffin bristling with thorns, which seemed to have been opened for me. I awoke in a state of terrible agitation; a multitude of confused feelings arose in my soul, and a secret voice seemed to say to me, "Yes, as long as you live, your poor victim will draw tears of blood from you which will become more agonizing every day, and the goad of your remorse will constantly grow sharper, rather than duller."

Such was the state in which I reached Nancy, monsieur. A thousand new sorrows were awaiting me there; once the hand of fate descends upon us, its blows increase until they crush us.

I went to visit Madame de Verquin; she had asked me to come in her last letter, and she had said that she was looking forward to seeing me, but little did I realize the conditions under which we were going to share the joy of seeing each other again. She was on her deathbed when I arrived. Merciful heaven, who would have thought it! She had written to me only

---

*The reader is invited to remember the expression "a woman who was unknown to me," in order to avoid confusion. Florville still has other losses to suffer before the veil is lifted and she is able to learn the identity of the woman she saw in her dream.

two weeks before, telling me of her present pleasures and announcing others to come. Such are the plans of mortals: it's while they're forming them, in the midst of their amusements, that merciless death comes to cut the thread of their days; living without ever concerning themselves with that fateful moment, as though they were going to be on earth forever, they vanish into the dark cloud of immortality, uncertain of the fate that lies in store for them.

Allow me, monsieur, to interrupt the story of my adventures a few moments to tell you about Madame de Verquin's death, and to describe to you the frightening stoicism which accompanied her to the grave.

After an escapade that was foolish for her age (she was then fifty-two), Madame de Verquin had jumped into the water to cool herself. She fainted and was brought home in an alarming state. Pneumonia set in the following day, and on the sixth day she was told that she had no more than twenty-four hours to live. This news didn't frighten her; she knew I was going to come, and she ordered that I be received.

I arrived on the very evening when, according to her doctor, she was going to die. She'd had herself placed in a room furnished with the greatest possible taste and elegance. She was lying, casually dressed, on a voluptuous bed whose lilac-colored silk curtains were pleasantly set off by garlands of natural flowers. Every corner was adorned by bouquets of carnations, jasmine, tuberoses and roses; she was pulling off the petals of some of them, and she'd already covered her bed and the whole room with them. She held out her hand to me as soon as she saw me.

"Come, Florville," she said, "embrace me on my bed of flowers. . . . How tall and beautiful you've become!

Ah, yes, my child, virtue has done you good. . . . You've been told about my condition . . . You've been told about it, Florville . . . I know about it too. . . . In a few hours I'll be gone; I'd never have thought I'd have so little time to spend with you when I saw you again. . . ."

She saw my eyes fill with tears. "Come, come, foolish girl," she said, "don't be childish. . . . Do you really think there's any reason to feel sorry for me? Haven't I had as much pleasure as any other woman in the world? I'm losing all the years when I'd have had to give up my pleasures, and what would I have done without them? The truth is that I don't pity myself at all for not living to be older than I am now. Before long, no man would have wanted me, and I've never had any desire to live to an age when I'd arouse repugnance. Only believers have any reason to fear death, my child; always between heaven and hell, not knowing which will open to receive them, they're torn by anxiety. As for me, I hope for nothing, and I'm sure of being no more unhappy after my death than I was before my life. I'm going to sleep peacefully in the bosom of nature, without regret or grief, without remorse or apprehension. I've asked to be buried in my bower of jasmine; my place is already being prepared in it. I'll be there, Florville, and the atoms that come from my disintegrating body will nourish the flowers I've loved most of all. And next year," she went on, stroking my cheek with a bouquet of those flowers, "when you smell them you'll be inhaling your dead friend's soul; the fragrance will force its way into the fibers of your brain, give you pleasant ideas and make you think of me."

My tears began to flow again. I clasped the hands of that unfortunate woman and tried to make her exchange her frightful materialistic ideas for a less impious view-point, but as soon as she became aware of my intention she pushed me away in alarm.

"Oh, Florville," she cried, "please don't poison my last moments with your errors! Let me die in peace. I hated those errors all my life, and I'm not going to adopt them now that I'm about to die."

I said nothing. What could my feeble eloquence have done against such firmness? I would only have distressed her without converting her; simple human kindness opposed it. She pulled her bell cord and I immediately heard sweet, melodious music which seemed to be coming from an adjoining room.

"This is how I intend to die, Florville," said that Epicurean. "Isn't it better than being surrounded by priests who would fill my last moments with turmoil, alarm and despair? No, I want to teach your pious believers that it's possible to die in peace without being like them. I want to convince them that it doesn't require religion, but only courage and reason."

Time was passing. A notary came in; she had sent for him. The music stopped. She dictated a few last wishes. She had no children and she had been a widow for a number of years, so she was able to dispose of many things as she saw fit; she left legacies to her friends and her servants. Then she took a little coffer from a writing desk near her bed.

"Here's all I have left now," she said, "a little cash and a few jewels. Let's amuse ourselves the rest of the evening. There are six of you in my room now; I'm going to divide all this into six parts and we'll have a lottery. Each one of you will keep whatever he wins."

I was amazed by her composure. It seemed incredible to me that she could have so many things with which to reproach herself, and yet approach her last moment with such calm—a pernicious effect of unbelief. If the horrible deaths of some wicked people make us shudder, how much more frightened we ought to be by such steadfast impenitence!

What she wanted was done. She had a magnificent meal served. She ate from several dishes and drank liqueurs and Spanish wines, for the doctor had told her that in her condition it didn't matter.

The lots were drawn and each of us received nearly two thousand francs in gold or jewels. This little game was scarcely over when she was seized with a violent attack.

"Well, is this it?" she asked the doctor, still with complete serenity.

"I'm afraid so, madame."

"Then come, Florville," she said, holding out her arms to me, "come and receive my last farewells. I want to die on the bosom of virtue...."

She clasped me tightly in her arms and her beautiful eyes closed forever.

Being a stranger in that house and no longer having any reason to stay there, I left immediately. I leave you to imagine the state I was in, and how much that spectacle still darkened my mind.

The gap between Madame de Verquin's way of thinking and mine was too great to allow me to love her with complete sincerity. Furthermore, she was the first cause of my dishonor and all the calamities that had followed it. And yet that woman, sister of the only man who had really taken care of me, had never treated me with anything but kindness, and had continued to do so even on her deathbed. My tears were therefore quite sincere, and their bitterness redoubled when I reflected that, with her excellent qualities, that miserable creature had involuntarily brought on her own perdition, and that, already cast out from God's bosom, she was no doubt painfully undergoing the punishment she had earned by her depraved life. However, the thought of God's supreme goodness came to soothe the distress that these ideas had caused in me. I fell to my knees and dared to pray the Almighty to forgive that unfortunate soul; even though I myself had great need of heaven's mercy, I dared to implore it for someone else. To sway heaven as much as was in my power, I added two hundred francs of my own money to what I had won in Madame de Verquin's lottery and had it all distributed among the poor of her parish.

Her last wishes were scrupulously respected; she had made her arrangements so well that they could not fail to be carried out. She was buried in her bower of jasmine. At her head was a black marble obelisk on which this single word was carved: *Vixit.*

Thus died the sister of my dearest friend. Full of intelligence and knowledge, richly endowed with charms and talents, Madame de Verquin could have deserved, if she had behaved differently, the love and esteem of all those who knew her; instead, she obtained only their contempt. Her licentiousness had increased as she grew older. Someone who has no principles is never more dangerous than at the age when he has ceased to blush: depravity corrupts his heart, he refines his first failings, and gradually he begins to commit crimes, thinking he is still only indulging in follies. But I was constantly surprised by the incredible blindness of Madame de Verquin's brother. Such is the distinctive mark of candor and goodness; virtuous people, never suspecting the evil of which they themselves are incapable, are readily taken in by the first scoundrel who seizes upon them, and that's why there's so much ease and so little glory in deceiving them. The insolent rogue who does it is only working to demean himself, and, without even proving his talent for vice, he only lends greater brilliance to virtue.

In losing Madame de Verquin, I'd also lost all hope of learning anything about my lover and my son; as you can well imagine, I hadn't dared to question her about them when I saw the terrible state she was in.

Crushed by this catastrophe and exhausted from a journey made in a painful state of mind, I decided to rest for a time in Nancy, at the inn where I already had a room, without seeing anyone at all, since Monsieur de Saint-Prât had seemed to want me to conceal my name. It was there that I wrote to my dear protector, having resolved not to leave until I'd received his answer:

> *A wretched girl who is nothing to you, mon-*
> *sieur, and who can lay claim only to your pity,*
> *endlessly troubles your life; instead of speaking*
> *to you only of the grief you must be feeling*
> *over the loss you have just suffered, she dares*
> *to speak to you of herself, to ask you for your*
> *orders and to await them . . .*

But it was ordained that misfortune was to follow me everywhere, and that I was to be constantly either a witness or a victim of its sinister effects.

One evening I came back to the inn rather late after having gone out for a breath of fresh air with my maid and a footman whom I had hired temporarily on arriving in Nancy. Everyone else had already gone to bed. As I was about to go into my room, a woman in her early fifties, tall and still beautiful, whom I'd known by sight since my arrival at the inn, suddenly came out of her room, next to mine, and, armed with a dagger, rushed into a room across the hall. My natural inclination was to see . . . I hurried forward, followed by my servants, and in the twinkling of an eye, before we had time to stop her or even call out to her, we saw that wretched woman throw herself on another woman, stab her in the heart a dozen times, then go back to her room in a frenzied state, without having seen us. We thought at first that she'd gone mad; we couldn't understand her crime, for which no motive was apparent to us. When I saw that my maid and my footman were about to cry out, an overpowering impulse, whose cause was unknown to me, made me order them to remain silent, seize them by the arm, pull them into my room and close the door behind us.

We soon heard a frightful commotion: the woman who had just been stabbed had managed to stagger to the head of the stairs, screaming horribly. Before she died she was able to name her murderer. Since it was known that we were the last to enter the inn, we were arrested at the same time as the murderer. However, since the victim's accusation had cast no suspicion on us, we were merely ordered not to leave the inn until the end of the trial.

The murderer was imprisoned, but she admitted nothing and firmly maintained that she was innocent. My servants and I were the only witnesses. We were summoned to testify. I had to speak, and I also had to conceal the agitation that was secretly devouring me. I deserved death as much as the woman my forced testimony was going to send to the scaffold, for although the circumstances had been different, I was guilty of the same crime. I would have given anything to avoid that cruel testimony. It seemed to me as I spoke that with each word a drop of blood was torn from my heart. But our statements had to be complete; we reported everything we had seen.

We later learned that no matter how firmly convinced the authorities may have been that the crime was committed by that woman, whose motive had been to do away with a rival, it would have been impossible to convict her if it hadn't been for us, because a man involved in the situation had fled and might have been suspected; but the poor woman's doom was sealed by our testimony—especially that of my footman, who happened to be attached to the inn where the crime had been committed—which we could not have refused to give without placing ourselves in danger.

The last time I confronted her, she examined me with great astonishment and asked me how old I was.

"I'm thirty-four," I replied.

"Thirty-four? . . . And you're from this province?"

"No, madame."

"Your name is Florville?"

"Yes, that's what I'm called."

"I don't know you," she said, "but you're an honest woman, and you're said to be respected in this town; unfortunately that's enough for me. . . . Mademoiselle," she went on with agitation, "I had a dream in which you appeared to me in the midst of the horrors that now surround me. You were there with my son . . . Yes, I'm a mother, and an unhappy one, as you can see. You had the same face, the same figure, the same dress . . . And the scaffold was before my eyes . . ."

"A dream," I exclaimed, "a dream, madame!" I immediately recalled my own dream, and I was struck by her features: I recognized her as the woman who had appeared to me with Senneval, near the coffin bristling with thorns. Tears welled up in my eyes. The more I examined that woman, the more I was tempted to retract my testimony. I wanted to ask to be executed in her stead, I wanted to flee and yet I couldn't tear myself away. . . .

Having no reason to doubt my innocence, the officials merely separated us when they saw the terrible state in which she'd placed me. I went back to my inn in despair, overwhelmed by a multitude of feelings whose cause I couldn't discern. The next day, that miserable woman was put to death.

On that same day I received Monsieur de Saint-Prât's answer. He urged me to come back. Nancy was, of course, no longer very pleasant to me, after the grim scenes it had just offered me, so I left it immediately and set out for Paris, pursued by the new ghost of that woman, who seemed to cry out to me at every moment, "It's you who've sent me to my death, wretched girl, and you don't know who it is that your own hand has pushed into the grave!"

Crushed by all these afflictions and persecuted by an equal number of sorrows, I asked Monsieur de Saint-Prât to find me a retreat in which I could end my days in the deepest solitude, and in the most rigorous duties of my religion. He suggested the one in which you found me, monsieur. I took up residence in it that same week, and from then on I left it only twice a month, to visit my dear protector and to spend a little time with Madame de Lérince. But heaven, which seems determined to deal me a painful blow every day, didn't let me enjoy my friendship with Madame de Lérince for long: I had the misfortune of losing her last year. Her affection for me required that I stay with her during those cruel moments, and she, too, breathed her last in my arms.

But who would have believed it, monsieur? Her death was less peaceful than Madame de Verquin's. Since Madame de Verquin had never hoped for anything, she wasn't afraid of losing everything. Madame de Lérince seemed to dread seeing the object of her hope disappear. I had noticed no remorse in Madame de Verquin, who should have been overwhelmed by it; Madame de Lérince, who had never given herself any reason for remorse, felt it keenly. At her death, Madame de Verquin regretted only that she hadn't done enough evil; Madame de Lérince died regretting the good she hadn't done. One covered herself with flowers and lamented only the loss of her pleasures, the other wanted to die on a cross of ashes, and was grieved by the memory of the hours she hadn't devoted to virtue.

I was struck by these contrasts. A little laxity stole over my soul. "Why," I said to myself, "isn't virtue rewarded with calm at that time, when it seems to be granted to misconduct?" But then, strengthened by a heavenly voice that seemed to thunder from the depths of my heart, I immediately cried out, "Is it for me to fathom God's will? What I see only assures me of one more merit. Madame de Lérince's fear was the solicitude of virtue; Madame de Verquin's cruel indifference was only the last aberration of crime. Ah, if I have a choice in my last moments, may God grant me the favor of frightening me like Madame de Lérince, rather than numbing me like Madame de Verquin!"

Such is the last of my adventures, monsieur. For the past two years I've been living at the Convent of the Assumption, where my benefactor placed me. Yes, monsieur, I've been living there for two years, and not once have I had a moment of rest, not once have I spent a night without seeing the image of poor Saint-Ange and the unfortunate woman whose execution I caused in Nancy. Now you know the state in which you found me, and the secret things I had to reveal to you. Wasn't it my duty to inform you of them before yielding to the feelings that had deceived you? Now you can see whether it's possible for me to be worthy of you, and whether a woman whose soul is torn by sorrow could bring any joy to your life. Take my advice, monsieur: stop deluding yourself, let me return to the stern seclusion which is the only kind of existence that befits me. If you were to tear me away from it, you would constantly have before your eyes the frightful spectacle of remorse, grief and misfortune.

By the time she had thus ended her story, Mademoiselle de Florville was in a state of violent agitation. Naturally animated, sensitive and delicate, she could not fail to be deeply affected by such a recital of her tribulations.

Monsieur de Courval did not feel that the later events of her story presented any more valid reasons for changing his plans than the earlier ones had done. He did everything he could to calm the woman he loved.

"Let me say again, mademoiselle," he said to her, "that there are fateful and singular things in what you've just told me, but that I don't see a single one that ought to alarm your conscience or damage your reputation. An affair at the age of sixteen, so be it, but there were many excuses on your side: your age, Madame de Verquin's efforts to lead you astray, a young man who was no doubt very charming . . . and whom you've never seen since then, have you, mademoiselle?" he added with a touch of anxiety. "And you'll probably never see him again . . ."

"Oh, certainly not!" said Florville, sensing the reasons for his anxiety.

"Well, then, mademoiselle," he said, "let's conclude our arrangements, I beg you, and let me convince you as soon as possible that there's nothing in your story that could diminish, in the heart of an honest man, either the consideration owed to all your virtues or the homage demanded by all your charms."

She asked for permission to return to Paris again to consult her protector for the last time, and promised that she would raise no further objections. He could not refuse to let her fulfill that virtuous duty. She left, and came back a week later with Saint-Prât. Monsieur de Courval showered courteous attentions on him; he made it abundantly clear to him how greatly flattered he was to be able to marry the girl he was kind enough to protect, and he begged him to go on acknowledging her as his relative. Saint-Prât responded graciously to Courval's attentions and continued to give him extremely advantageous notions concerning Mademoiselle de Florville's character.

At last came the day that Courval had desired so much. The ceremony took place, and when the contract was read he was surprised to learn that, without telling anyone, Monsieur de Saint-Prât had, in consideration of Florville's marriage, doubled the income of four thousand francs a year which he was already giving her, and bequeathed her a hundred thousand francs to be paid to her after his death.

She shed abundant tears when she saw her protector's new kindnesses to her, and at the bottom of her heart she was glad to be able to offer the man who was good enough to marry her a fortune at least equal to his own.

Cordiality, pure joy and reciprocal assurances of esteem and attachment presided over the celebration of that wedding ... of that fateful wedding whose torches were secretly extinguished by the Furies.

Monsieur de Saint-Prât spent a week in Courval's country house, along with our bridegroom's friends, but the newlyweds did not return to Paris with them: they decided to stay in the country until the beginning of winter, to give themselves time to put their affairs in order so that they would be able to establish a good household in Paris. Monsieur de Saint-Prât was instructed to find them a pleasing residence near his own, to enable them to see each other more often.

Monsieur and Madame de Courval had already spent nearly three months together in the sweet anticipation of all those agreeable arrangements, and they were already certain of her pregnancy, which they had hastened to announce to the good Monsieur de Saint-Prât, when an unexpected event blighted the well-being of the happy couple and changed the tender roses of wedlock into the mournful cypresses of sorrow.

At this point my pen stops. . . . I ought to ask my readers for mercy, beg them to go no further ... Yes, let them stop immediately if they do not wish to shudder with horror. . . . Sad condition of mankind on earth, cruel effects of the capriciousness of fate ... Why should the unhappy Florville, the most virtuous, charming and sensitive girl in the world, have found herself, through an almost inconceivable series of fateful events, the most abominable monster that nature could have created?

One evening that tender, loving wife was sitting beside her husband, reading an incredibly gloomy

English novel which was causing a great stir at the time.

"There's someone who's almost as unfortunate as I am," she said, throwing down the book.

"As unfortunate as you?" said Monsieur de Courval, clasping his beloved wife in his arms. "Oh, Florville, I thought I'd made you forget your misfortunes! I see I was mistaken. . . . Did you have to say it to me so harshly?"

But Madame de Courval had become as though insensitive: she did not even utter a word in response to his caresses. With an involuntary movement, she pushed him away in alarm, hurried over to a sofa, lay down on it and burst into tears. It was in vain that the worthy Courval threw himself at the feet of the woman he worshiped and begged her either to calm herself or at least tell him the cause of her sudden despair. She continued to repulse him and turn away from him when he tried to dry her tears, until finally, no longer doubting that a pernicious memory of her former passion had come to inflame her anew, he could not help reproaching her a little on the subject.

For a time she listened to him without answering, then she stood up and said, "No, monsieur, you're mistaken in giving that interpretation to the sorrow that overwhelmed me just now. I'm frightened not by memories, but by forebodings. . . . I see myself happy with you, monsieur—yes, very happy—and I wasn't born for happiness. It's impossible for me to go on like this much longer: my destiny is such that the dawn of happiness is always the lightning which precedes a thunderbolt. . . . That's what makes me shudder: I'm afraid we weren't destined to live together. Perhaps tomorrow I shall no longer be your wife. . . . A secret voice cries out from the depths of my heart that all this happiness is only a shadow which is about to vanish like a flower that springs up and is cut down in a single day. So don't accuse me of being capricious or becoming cold toward you, monsieur: I'm guilty only of excessive sensibility and an unhappy tendency to see everything in its most sinister aspect—a painful result of my afflictions. . . ."

Monsieur de Courval was still at her feet, unsuccessfully trying to calm her by his caresses and his words, when suddenly (it was about seven o'clock on an evening in October) a servant came in to say that a stranger was insistently asking to speak to Monsieur de Courval. Florville shuddered. Involuntary tears streamed down her cheeks, her legs became unsteady and she sat down; she tried to speak, but her voice died on her lips.

More concerned with his wife's condition than with what his servant had just told him, Monsieur de Courval curtly ordered him to tell the visitor to wait, then he hurried to Florville's aid. But, afraid of succumbing to the secret emotion that was gripping her, and wishing to hide her feelings from the stranger whose arrival had been announced, she stood up forcefully and said, "It's nothing, monsieur, it's nothing . . . Let the gentleman come in."

The servant left and returned a moment later, followed by a man thirty-seven or thirty-eight years old whose face, though quite attractive, bore the marks of a deeply rooted sorrow.

"Father!" cried the stranger, throwing himself at Monsieur de Courval's feet. "Will you recognize a wretched man who's been separated from you for twenty-two years, and who's been all too severely punished for his cruel misconduct by the calamities that have constantly overwhelmed him ever since he left you?"

"What! You're my son? Good heavens! ... By what event ... Ingrate! What made you remember my existence?"

"My heart ... that heart which has never stopped loving you, despite its guilt. ... Listen to me, father, I have greater misfortunes than my own to reveal to you; please sit down and hear me. And you, madame," continued young Courval, turning to his father's wife, "please forgive me if, immediately after paying my respects to you for the first time in my life, I'm forced to relate some terrible family catastrophes which it's no longer possible to conceal from my father."

"Speak, monsieur, speak," stammered Madame de Courval, looking at him with haggard eyes, "the language of unhappiness isn't new to me: I've known it ever since my childhood."

Staring at her with a kind of involuntary agitation, the young man said to her, "You've been unhappy, madame? Ah, merciful heaven, can you have been as unhappy as we?"

They sat down. Madame de Courval's state would be difficult to describe. She glanced at the visitor, looked down at the floor, sighed from inner turmoil. Monsieur de Courval was weeping while his son tried to calm him and begged him to lend him his attention. Finally the conversation took a more orderly turn.

"I have so many things to tell you, monsieur," said young Courval, "that you'll have to allow me to omit the details and tell you only the main facts. And I want you and madame to give me your word not to interrupt me until I've finished.

"I left you when I was fifteen, monsieur. My first impulse was to go to my mother, whom I was blind enough to prefer to you. She'd been separated from you for many years. I rejoined her in Lyons. Her scandalous life alarmed me so much that I had to flee from her to preserve what remained of the sentiments I owed to her. I went to Strasbourg, where the Normandy regiment was garrisoned . . ."

Madame de Courval started, but controlled herself.

"My colonel took a certain interest in me," young Courval went on. "I attracted his attention and he made me a second lieutenant. The following year, I went with the regiment to Nancy, where I fell in love with Madame de Verquin's young niece. I seduced her, had a son by her, then cruelly abandoned her."

At these words, Madame de Courval quivered and a low moan escaped from her chest, but she continued to be firm.

"That wretched adventure was the cause of all my misfortunes. I placed the poor girl's child in the home of a woman who lived near Metz, and who promised to take care of him. A short time later I returned to my regiment. My conduct was strongly condemned. Since the young lady hadn't been able to reappear in Nancy, I was accused of having ruined her. Too charming not to have interested the whole town, she found avengers there. I fought a duel, killed my adversary and went to Turin with my son, after going back to Metz to get him.

"I spent twelve years in the service of the King of Sardinia. I won't describe the mishaps I encountered there; they were countless. It's only by leaving France that one learns to miss it. Meanwhile my son was growing and showing great promise. I became acquainted in

Turin with a French lady who had accompanied one of our princesses who married into that court. When this respectable lady took an interest in my misfortunes, I ventured to ask her to take my son to France so that he could finish his education there. I promised her that I would order my affairs well enough to be able to come and take him from her care in six years. She consented, took my poor child to Paris, spared no effort to give him a good upbringing, and regularly sent me news of him.

"I came a year earlier than I'd promised. I went to the lady's house, filled with the sweet expectation of embracing my son, of holding in my arms that token of a sentiment which I had betrayed, but which still burned in my heart. . . . 'Your son is no longer living,' my worthy friend said to me with tears in her eyes. 'He was a victim of the same passion that brought such unhappiness to his father. We'd taken him to the country. He fell in love there with a charming girl whose name I've sworn not to reveal. Carried away by the violence of his love, he tried to take by force what she'd refused him out of virtue. . . . She stabbed him, intending only to frighten him, but she pierced his heart and he fell dead. . . .'"

At this point Madame de Courval fell into a kind of stupor which for a moment made the two men fear that she had suddenly lost her life. Her eyes were glazed, her pulse had stopped. Monsieur de Courval, who was all too clearly aware of the appalling way in which those deplorable events were related, told his son to be silent and hurried to his wife. She regained consciousness and said with heroic courage, "Let your son go on, monsieur. Perhaps I haven't yet reached the end of my afflictions."

Not understanding her sorrow over events that seemed to concern her only indirectly, but discerning something incomprehensible in her face, young Courval looked at her with emotion. Monsieur de Courval took his son's hand and, after distracting his attention from Florville, told him to go on with his story without dwelling on any unnecessary details, for it contained mysterious circumstances that were of the greatest interest.

"In despair over the death of my son," continued young Courval, "and no longer having anything to hold me in France—except you, father, but I didn't dare to approach you and I dreaded your anger—I decided to travel to Germany. . . . Ill-fated father, I still haven't told you the most painful part of my story," he said, wetting his father's hands with his tears. "I beg you to summon up your courage.

"When I arrived in Nancy I learned that a Madame Desbarres—this was the name my mother had adopted in her disorderly life, as soon as she had made you believe she was dead—had just been imprisoned for having stabbed her rival to death, and that she was perhaps going to be executed the next day."

"Oh, monsieur!" exclaimed poor Florville, throwing herself in her husband's arms with tears and heartrending cries. "Oh, monsieur, do you see the full extent of my afflictions?"

"Yes, madame, I see everything," said Monsieur de Courval, "but please let my son finish."

Florville restrained herself, but she had almost stopped breathing, all her feelings were impaired, and all her muscles were frightfully taut.

"Go on, my son, go on," said the unhappy father. "In a few minutes I'll explain everything to you."

"Well, monsieur," said young Courval, "I made inquiries to see if there was any confusion of names. I found that it was unfortunately all too true that the criminal was my mother. I asked to see her and my request was granted. I threw myself into her arms. 'I'm going to die guilty,' the poor woman said to me, 'but there's a terrible stroke of fate in the events that have led me to my death. A certain man was going to be suspected of my crime, and he would have been, because all the evidence was against him, but a woman and her two servants who happened to be in the inn saw me commit the murder, and I was so preoccupied that I didn't notice them. Their testimony was the sole cause of my death sentence. But no matter; I have only a little time left to talk to you, and I don't want to waste it on futile complaints. I have some important secrets to tell you; listen to them, my son.'

" 'As soon as my eyes are closed, go to my husband and tell him that among all my crimes there's one which he never knew, and which I finally confessed. . . . You have a sister, Courval. She was born a year after you. I adored you and I was afraid she would be a drawback to you some day because your father might make a dowry for her by taking some of the money you would inherit. To keep it intact for you, I decided to get rid of my daughter and do everything in my power to make sure my husband would have no more children from our marriage. My disorders led me into other failings and forestalled the effect of those new crimes by making me commit other and more terrible ones; but as for my daughter, I mercilessly resolved to kill her. I was about to carry out that infamous plan, acting in concert with the wet nurse, whom I had amply compensated, when she told me that she knew a man who had been married for many years and constantly wanted children without being able to have them, and that she could rid me of my daughter without committing a crime, and in a way that might give her a happy life. I quickly accepted. That same night my daughter was left on the doorstep of that man with a note in her bassinet. As soon as I'm dead, hurry to Paris and beg your father to forgive me, not to curse my memory, and to claim his daughter for his own.'

"With these words, my mother kissed me and tried to calm the frightful agitation into which I'd been plunged by what she'd just told me. . . . Father, she was executed the next day. Then a terrible illness nearly put me in my grave; for two years I hovered between life and death, with neither the strength nor the courage to write to you. The first use I've made of my recovered health has been to come and throw myself at your feet, to beg you to forgive my unfortunate mother, and to give you the name of the man who can tell you what has become of my sister: he's Monsieur de Saint-Prât."

Monsieur de Courval was deeply perturbed; all his senses were frozen, he nearly lost consciousness, his condition became alarming.

As for Florville, who had been torn to pieces for the past quarter of an hour, she stood up with the serenity of someone who has just come to a decision and said to Courval, "Well, monsieur, now do you believe that a more horrible criminal than the wretched Florville can exist anywhere in the world? Recognize me, Senneval, recognize me as your sister, the girl you seduced in Nancy, your son's murderer, your father's wife, and the infamous creature who led your mother to the scaffold. . . . Yes, gentlemen, those are my crimes. When I look at either of you I see an object of horror;

I either see my lover in my brother, or my husband in my father. And if I look at myself, I see only the abominable monster who stabbed her son and caused her mother's death. Do you think the Almighty can have enough torments for me? And do you think I can go on living any longer with the afflictions that are torturing my heart? No, I still have one more crime to commit, and it will avenge all the others."

The poor girl immediately leapt forward, snatched one of Senneval's pistols and shot herself in the head before either of the two men had time to realize her intention. She died without saying another word.

Monsieur de Courval fainted. His son, dazed by those horrible scenes, called for help as best he could. Florville no longer had any need for assistance: the shadows of death had already spread over her brow, and her features had been doubly contorted by the throes of despair and the upheaval of a violent death. She lay in a pool of her own blood.

Monsieur de Courval was carried to his bed. He was at death's door for two months. His son, in an equally painful state, was nevertheless fortunate enough to see his affection and care bring back his father's health. But after all the blows which fate had so cruelly rained down upon their heads, they decided to withdraw from the world. Austere solitude has taken them from their friends forever, and now, in the bosom of piety and virtue, each of them is peacefully finishing a sad and oppressive life which was given to him only to convince him, as well as those who will read this tragic story, that it is only in the darkness of the tomb that man can find the calm which the wickedness of his fellow man, the disorder of his passions, and, above all, the decrees of his fate, will always refuse to him on this earth.

Bantam Classics bring you the world's greatest literature—books that have stood the test of time—at specially low prices. These beautifully designed books will be proud additions to your bookshelf. You'll want all these time-tested classics for your own reading pleasure.

Titles by Mark Twain:

☐ 21079-3	**ADVENTURES OF HUCKLEBERRY FINN**	$2.50
☐ 21128-5	**ADVENTURES OF TOM SAWYER**	$2.25
☐ 21195-1	**COMPLETE SHORT STORIES**	$5.95
☐ 21143-9	**A CONNECTICUT YANKEE IN KING ARTHUR'S COURT**	$3.50
☐ 21349-0	**LIFE ON THE MISSISSIPPI**	$2.50
☐ 21256-7	**THE PRINCE AND THE PAUPER**	$2.25
☐ 21158-7	**PUDD'NHEAD WILSON**	$2.50

Other Great Classics:

☐ 21274-5	**BILLY BUDD** Herman Melville	$2.95
☐ 21311-3	**MOBY DICK** Herman Melville	$3.50
☐ 21233-8	**THE CALL OF THE WILD & WHITE FANG** Jack London	$2.95
☐ 21011-4	**THE RED BADGE OF COURAGE** Stephen Crane	$1.95
☐ 21350-4	**THE COUNT OF MONTE CRISTO** Alexander Dumas	$4.95

Bantam Books, Dept. CL2, 2451 South Wolf Road, Des Plaines, IL 60018

Please send me the items I have checked above. I am enclosing $_____ (please add $2.50 to cover postage and handling). Send check or money order, no cash or C.O.D.s please.

Mr/Ms _____

Address _____

City/State _____ Zip _____

CL2-5/93

Please allow four to six weeks for delivery.
Prices and availability subject to change without notice.